AF426583

Trigger Warning:

Reader discretion is advised; this book contains material that may be triggering to some audiences, such as the following: mentions of death and the process of dying, mental health disorders, mentions and descriptions of suicide, and mentions and descriptions of abortion. I value your mental health, if at any point, any of the content is affecting you, please put the book down.

DEDICATION:

To those who tried to leave and are still here, there is always someone willing to fight for you. And, to my sister who has held my hand even when I don't ask her to.

Rogue Reaper
A Fight for Life in Death
P.R. Miguel

CHAPTER 1

O pal opens her eyes, an unfamiliar atmosphere glitters around her like a thousand suns. She stands at the center of the universe, and before her are three mighty giants; above them, Earth hovers, witnessing as she takes in the sight.

"Where am I?" She asks, her hands patting her face.

"Opal Tempest–step onto the podium to receive your judgment."

The figure in the center rises from its seat. It has the silhouette of a lady, slender curves, and soft lines. There are two equally giant figures seated in their respective thrones beside her. Although they are not distinguishable by characteristics, they are undoubtedly male.

"Judgment?" She whispers.

A long, opaque path forms at her feet, leading her up towards a podium, standing at eye level with the Gods. With a held breath, her feet drag her all the way up to where she stands. There she holds the gaze of three sets of eyes, reading her inside and out.

"Opal, the judgment of your life is nullified, you have committed the most unforgivable sin, and are condemned to one hundred

Earth years of Reaper service and an eternity in the Underworld when finished." The feminine shadow says.

The biggest sin, she said. Bewilderment at the accusations. What crime? What sin could she have possibly committed? How does one crime atone for the nullification of her judgment?

"What did I do?" Her hands tremble at the insinuation that she is, in fact, dead. And, in front of her stands God themselves.

"Taking a life, specifically your own, is a non-pardonable sin." A thunderous male voice emanates from the figure to the right. Behind him, there is a single wing framing his bulky figure, glimmering ever so slightly under the dim starlight and through the veil of shadow that hides the three of them.

"Suicide? I–I don't remember." Opal stutters.

"Life is a sacred gift, it is not to be taken, especially by your own hands. Under the law that rules this realm and the one you resided in previously, it is inexcusable." The figure to the left says softly as it takes a crunching bite from a fruit. Upon closer inspection, through the squinting of her eyes, he seems to be wearing a crown-shaped headpiece with exactly six points. The red from his irises is so bright that they were easily detectable even through the blanket of darkness that kept them hidden from her.

"You have no rights here, dear. There is nothing to be done. Please step off the podium and begin your sentence." Her voice, so silky it lingers in Opal's head.

Despite the beautiful setting displayed ahead, she can not find a moment to appreciate the sights. She is too busy feeling everything and nothing at the same time: her hands feel clammy, but there is no sweat, and her head thunders at the same beat of her non-existent heart. She turns away from the three Gods and begins her descent back down; there is someone already waiting for her at the base.

A cloaked entity holding the wooden base of its scythe. Floating, or hovering effortlessly. It doesn't peel its hood to acknowledge her or hold out a hand in greeting. It was safe under the cloak, and it kept it that way as Opal approached it.

"Wait." She objects before her foot steps off the pathway.

"It's not fair!"

The Reaper's head tilts up, being captivated by the grandness of the girl at the fore and her tenacity to question the Gods, who are now standing. All three note the defiance in her tone.

During her life on Earth, she was rarely the kind of person who resigned without questioning; her afterlife would be no different. However, most of her approaches were head-on, and here she didn't have a clue what true power was and that she held none of it, not even in this moment.

"The reason is beyond your unworthy mind, *human*." The gold in his feathers shimmers with the vibration of his loud voice.

A court seemingly in space, with three judges holding a trial for someone they already deem guilty. The situation didn't sit right with her. She looks at them, studies their shadows, and the thrones they sit in. Simple and yet ornate seats, unlike them, their thrones are perfectly visible. They were made of resplendent materials: one white, one silver, one gold. They are plain with sharp edges and no intricate embossings or details, but grand enough to help Opal realize that her best option was to serve her sentence and deal with it. Her fate was out of her hands.

"Deus, manners." The female scolds softly, her voice stern and effectively sitting Deus down.

Opal can't distinguish their features, but despite that, their authority and power radiate from them. When her back turns away from them, she feels their stares burn through her skull. She shifts her focus to the Reaper ahead, floating so delicately and lifelessly. She notices how it follows all orders without hesitation. In that moment, she sees her future.

"It's futile to fight. I don't understand what's happening. How did this happen?" She thinks to herself, throwing one last glance at the Gods behind her, who still watch her every move.

In an environment she knows nothing about, she holds the disadvantage, but not for lack of trying.

CHAPTER 2

She follows the Reaper down a single hallway. The coffee colored cloak covers its face and broad shoulders. She feels his hyper-awareness.

Opal keeps her eyes trained on the ground while she waits for the opportunity to freak out. How did it happen? How did she do it? When did she do it? An avalanche of questions floods her mind, and without any clear answers, she changes her focus to the being next to her.

"You're um...a Reaper, right? What's your name?" She asks.

He didn't respond. When she spoke, he couldn't help but close his eyes at the sound of her voice and guiltily enjoy her timbre. It was a lovely sound, unlike the voices of the other newcomers he oriented, and uncertain of what reaction she elicited from him. He shuffles through his memory, sure that he hasn't felt his chest thud like that in years, after decades of being literally heartless. He found it difficult to keep his composure and opted for the comfort of silence instead.

Opal thinks of the moment when a single swing of his scythe opened a rift, a fracture between two places: a portal. They stepped through, and the portal effectively shut behind them. Not a word has been said since.

"Where are we going?" She asks. Still no response.

"How long have I been dead?" She continues.

The Reaper couldn't stall any longer. He wanted to answer, but it wasn't time yet. He wasn't allowed to give direction or reassurance until their training began. More importantly, he doesn't remember how to comfort someone. He doesn't remember how to be human.

She almost swore when he stopped abruptly, like a statue suspended in midair. No wonder they were called Reapers, and to think she will be carrying the same gloom to her drift soon. His arm extends to the right and points to a small walkway leading to a black door.

"You really expect me to walk through *that*?" She nods her head towards the walkway, which was more like a suspended bridge being held up by imaginary support.

The Reaper simply points in emphasis, avoiding as much contact as possible.

"Could you answer me?" she tugs on his sleeve, the material rough on her fingers.

He brushes her off, startled by the dauntless contact. Surprisingly, leaving him curious and longing for more of it. It had been years since his skin or even his cloak brushed against someone else.

"She's...odd." He thinks.

He ventures to look at her, amazed by the way she is processing all of this. Every other newcomer would be in tears or in full shock by now, instead all she wants are answers. Her eyes were still full of life, snapping him out of the small trance. He dares to touch her and gently push her towards the walkway. He stays still, waiting for her to take her next steps onto the suspended, stone bridge.

Moving forward, the floor felt sturdy under her feet, without rails or walls to hold on to. One foot after another, she extends her arms for balance. Her fingers brushed the space, desperately trying to catch a breeze, but there was nothing. With her chest threatening to crumble, she rushes the last few steps and reaches for the door.

He waited a second after her door closed. Something, there was something special about this girl, and he couldn't wait to find out what it was.

Inside: a small wooden bench, one pillow, and a blanket are backed against a stone wall. On the left side, a hook is suspended on the wall with her own cloak hanging from it, matching the one she saw on the Reaper outside.

"At least this place has walls." She sighs.

Opal lies quietly, assuming the bench will serve as her bed. The room is more like a cell than a suite; even so, it is the safest she has felt since she arrived in this realm. The concept of time was ambiguous here. To Opal, it felt like the longest day, and her body ached to its core. She rests herself on the hard bench, resting her head on the thin pillow. Without protest, she finally lets the tears spill from her eyes, rhythmically drumming against the bench, lulling her to sleep.

The wails of a horn blast in the small space, startling her awake. Rubbing her eyes, confused and unsure of how long she had been sleeping. Her eyes roam the room in an attempt to locate the source of the sound. Next to the cloak, a countdown displays on the wall in bright red numbers: a hologram. She isn't aware of what number it began, now she has exactly ten seconds to figure things out. There is only one thing to do after all.

Her hands reach for the coarse cloak and throws it on. She gets slightly tangled between the layers and the hood. Her long, cascading brown hair ends up tucked snuggly inside. The fabric tents over her body, allowing no feminine appeal to show. Underneath it, her linen clothes transform into a matching leather-like suit.

The countdown hits one, and the door flies open. She feels a pull in her chest, leading the way. The surroundings outside her room look just as she remembers and slowly become lit with soft candlelight. The pull is stronger as she approaches an opening into a large and circular room. With dull cement covering the walls of the chamber, and in the center, one single floating Reaper. Its scythe sits diagonally across its back.

He watches as she approaches the room. His chest feels a pull towards her. He fights it.

"You're a Reaper, pull it together. You have trained countless people. She isn't special." He tries to convince himself.

Her feet move as in their own accord, stopping a few feet away from him. Her eyes rise and fall, intently studying the being at her front.

He studies her right back when his shaky hand pulls back his hood. Beneath it, he reveals: an angular bone structure, dark wispy mid-length hair, prominent thick eyebrows framing his extensively discolored under eyes. His sharp nose turns down as he watches her reaction.

She openly stares, with her mouth slightly agape, noticing how his lips sit in an eternal frown. He looks in his early thirties, likely the time he forfeited his life.

"Tell me your name now." She demands, although softly.

She challenges him with her arms crossed when her eyes catch the prominent red scar around the circumference of his exposed neck. She notes the rough ridges and the various tones of pinks, reds, and purples decorating him like a necklace.

"Judas." He responds. "I will show you how to work your sentence. After three days, you're on your own." His voice is low and hoarse.

There is no hint of a smile or any emotion. His dark brown eyes don't sparkle either. He barely looks present.

"Judas...Just Judas?" Opal chews on the name.

"Judas Escarot." He replies.

They both stand in a silent duel, knowing exactly why they are both there. A muddy silence lingers between them until their eyes meet. He looks away quickly as if he saw a ghost and clears his throat.

"I will allow three questions about me, that was your first." His brow furrowed.

"Why did you commit suicide?" She asks bluntly.

"Of all questions, that's what you ask?" Sass drips from his tone. His hand runs through his hair, whilst he takes a deep breath to no relief since there is no air around them. She patiently waits for him to respond, understanding the weight of her question.

"It's simple. I betrayed my friend, my teacher. He was a good man and did not deserve it. He claimed that my actions were written, but in my heart, I knew I did it out of self-preservation. Returning the gold I received for my betrayal did not feel as proper punishment when my actions resulted in his cruel death. I now bear the marks of my actions around my neck as a daily reminder of what I did and why I deserve to be here." His hand encases his neck and rubs at his scar.

"Do you think this is fair?" She continues, noting how uncomfortable her previous question made him. At the same time, Opal searches her arms and roams her neck, trying to find evidence of how she took her own life.

"What I think is irrelevant. This is how things are and what I deserve."

Judas nods. Opal returns the gesture. Her opportunity to interview him is over, and poking him with personal questions was the least of her worries. In his head, he was hoping to prolong this moment. He felt aggravated and embarrassed by his past, and yet he hoped she would ask more. Unaware of his disappointment, she doesn't, as far more serious matters lie ahead of them, like the rest of her afterlife.

CHAPTER 3

There is a small chair against the wall. Judas hovers to it and places it in the center of the room.

"Sit." He says.

Opal inspects the chair, tests its stability, and finally does as she is told. Observing every move he makes as he pulls a chalkboard from the other side of the room. Her eyelid ticks when she realizes her first day in the afterlife would be attending a crash course on Reaping for beginners.

"Pay attention, I'm only running through this lesson once. Then we will go into didactics. On the second day, you will shadow me, and on the third, I will supervise as you Reap. Understood?"

He follows that with an uninterrupted, long tangent, while she absorbs the brief history lesson with only mild boredom. What did keep her attention was the way his hair swayed with each movement of his head, but no matter how long she admired him, her eyes kept being drawn to the scar on his neck.

"Deus is the God of light, ruler of Paradise. Dannato is the God of the damned, ruler of the Underworld. Parity is the God of balance, ruler of Purgatory. Together, they make the Oligarchy of the afterlife." She chews on her cheek as she tries to connect the dots during the information overload.

"Is it really necessary to have orientation?" Opal asks.

"Pointless questions at the end. As I was saying, Earth was created by the three of them, and there are three dimensions. The first dimension is Earth, which is where humans live. The second is Cielo, the afterlife, including all of the Gods' respective dominions. Lastly, the third dimension is Medio; it is sort of a third space. It's not here nor there, more like an in between." Judas lectures.

"That doesn't make any sense." She rolls her eyes with each syllable.

"It doesn't need to make sense. Medio is not ruled by the Gods, and other entities roam those grounds freely. We will discuss that later, though."

He continues lecturing, talking, and rambling about the role of Reapers in the afterlife. He moves his hands when he speaks so passionately about the rules. He catches how she occasionally dozes off while looking at him, which he brushes off to avoid the flush in his cheeks. He becomes weirdly self-conscious of the way she looks at him, only a tad mesmerized by her almond-shaped eyes.

"Reapers lead all lives to judgment, no matter the cause of death. We cut soul ties that attach humans to the Earth realm and safely navigate them to Cielo, to their judgment. We follow one simple law." He levels his eyes at her, effectively downturning his nose.

"The law of the Reaper is that we do not interfere." He finalizes.

After she readjusted in the small chair multiple times throughout what felt like hours of lecture. He joins his palms as in prayer.

"This part of the lecture has concluded." He sighs.

"When will I learn about...well, you know?" Her shoulders sag in hopes that he will understand what she is implying. It weighed heavily on her mind. She wanted to know exactly how it happened and what happened when she decided to take her own life.

"We earn it. It's an incentive to keep Reaping. Sometimes not knowing is better afterall. Some of us wish to forget, others long for the truth. In the end, we are all on the same boat to the Underworld regardless of what we want." Judas hovers to the center of the chamber, clearing the board in preparation for didactics.

CHAPTER 4

She itches with the cloak, scratching against her with the rough burlap material, prickling her skin raw. This whole room, dimly lit while Opal sat and listened intently, absorbing as much content as she could. Constantly readjusting in the small chair, barely able to sit still.

Judas, on the other hand, continues obsessing over the board and his artful stickfigure representing the anatomy of a scythe. His effort was appreciated by Opal, but his art skills are questionable.

He focused on the lecture. The latter would be to focus on her, and the way her grandeur stirred him in a way he had long forgotten. He cleared his throat when the drawing on the chalkboard was finally to his liking.

"The base," he pointed to it with his finger, "is made of wood for a good grip. Each movement has a specific purpose, and they are not to be played around with." He scolds, noting how trouble sizzles in her irises. "The blade," he traces the edge of the drawing with his index finger, "some of us call it the beak, is meant for severing soul ties to Earth and occasionally defense from Rogues."

"Okay…What are Rogues? And, where do I get one?" She asks.

"You have a relentless amount of questions." He throws her a glance as he unstraps his scythe from his back, bringing it forward. He grasps the base with both hands and tears an identical copy out from the original, effectively holding two scythes in his hands.

"Did you just copy and paste that?" Opal's jaw falls to the ground.

"What is copy and paste?" He scratches his head with a scowl. Judas watches as she stands and takes the lead as the teacher.

"You must be really old if you don't know what copy and paste is." She grabs the chalk, while he stands back and watches her draw an object he does not recognize. "This is a laptop. Others call it a computer. Copy and paste is a feature in these devices that allows you to copy an item, like a photo, and paste it into another file or location. Something like that." She points to the twin scythes he holds upright, resting the base of each one on the floor.

"Earth has changed so much since I was around. Catch!" He throws the weapon to her, for him it's light as a feather, for her it's the weight of a whole person.

He runs through the hand placement and movement sequences of scythe-wielding. She learns how to open rifts to Medio and back. She practices cutting soul ties and completes a strenuous shoulder exercise at the end of the lesson. She melts into the chair, holding her scythe upright with the base resting on the floor. When her hand touches it, there is a small flow of energy between the weapon and her. It sends small shockwaves and the tiniest vibrations, like it's saying hello.

"If I'm dead, why do I already feel sore?" She whines.

"You *are* dead, but feeling corporal aches is part of our sentence. That is also why we are allowed to sleep." He appreciates how she sprawls so freely onto the chair, making it look comfortable.

"Anyways, let's discuss the Rogues." He adds.

Opal is still planted on the chair, the same chair that gave her a backache during the first part of the lesson. She found that the scythe mounts itself on her back, as a work of magic. The weight of it, however, did not magically go away, pulling her shoulders back and her posture straight.

"Rogues are creatures, entities that are born from human nature, specifically self-inflicted death. Most manifest on Earth with other names, some of the most common include: Depression, Anxiety, PTSD, and more. In some cases, they can also take the form of strong negative emotions: Wrath, Envy, Rage, and so on, and so on." He rubs at his jaw.

"Wait, wait, wait…You are telling *me* that these so-called Rogues," she air quotes, "are actual entities that plague humans, pushing them to commit suicide?"

"Yes, I know, but the law–"

"I know the law! The law of the Reaper is that we don't interfere, blah, blah, blah… But, why don't *they* interfere?" She points up, glaring at the Gods through the pebbled ceiling that covers the circular chamber.

"Rogues live outside their dominion. They are created because of us, and they don't follow anyone's command but their own. The Gods deem it a test for the sanctity of life. People who succumb to set persuasion," he points to Opal and then himself, "are unworthy of trial because *we* are weak, and let's be honest, it is justified. Besides, interfering with Rogues is considered interfering with death according to the Gods."

"How do you know if we deserve it if we don't even get a trial? A judgement? How is any of this fair?" She demands answers, answers he isn't able to give.

Judas stands, a chill running down his back, while he observes her outburst. "She's right," he thought, "but there is nothing we can do about it." They take a moment to cool down in silence. He notices how the outrage in her facial expression melts away slowly, and only when it looked almost disseminated he continued to lecture.

"On the rare occasion a Rogue attacks you, like I said, rare occasion," he emphasizes, "you are to use the third and fourth movements." He demonstrates them and then allows her a moment to practice.

Opal stands, pulling the heavy weapon from her back. She nestles her hands close together in the center of the wooden pole. Her fists sit thumb to pinky. The beak of the blade faces outward. Her body sways with the first vertical chop and swiftly transitions to a horizontal swing: drawing a cross in the air. Her movements are delayed and slow, but with practice, she adjusts to the weight of her weapon.

"You'll get better with practice. That was the third movement, which will freeze the Rogue, preventing us from interfering too much, but it also prevents our second death." An odd chuckle escapes from him.

"A pathetic attempt at a joke, but please elaborate." She folds her arms while she recovers. To her surprise, she needs to catch her breath, an oddity since she owns no lungs and there is no air.

"It's not possible for us to die a second time, but to my understanding, our sentence restarts if we are defeated."

"This place is royally fucked up." She adds, gearing herself for the next move.

The fourth movement requires more skill and precision. Opal fails to perform it during their didactic, meaning that she will now be obsessing over it until she gets it perfectly. She studied how Judas placed his feet together while he hovered. His arms and broad shoulders work together, swirling the wooden handle of the scythe with one hand, creating a large, deadly fan. She distinguishes how his brow bunches in concentration, and only after snapping herself out of the moment, she acknowledges that to him, this was now second nature.

"The fourth movement will kill the Rogue. The goal is to avoid that at all costs. We are not meant to interfere with their affairs either. They also can't leave Medio, so if you are unsuccessful with your movements, you can always rift back to Cielo. Fair warning, leaving a death unreaped comes with punishment, usually in the form of a longer sentence."

"Great, because how else would they punish us? We're already going to hell."

"Dannato is known to be a fair ruler. He weighs your punishment in accordance with the weight of your sins and soul. Considering we didn't get a judgment, I'm not sure I personally want to find out what that means for an unpardonable sin. So...some of us may or may not add years to our sentence willingly." Judas shrugs.

CHAPTER 5

The loud wails of the same horn startle Opal awake. Dread weighs on her shoulders as she flays herself off the hard bench. She sits and studies her room, the red numbers, her scythe, and finally her cloak. Her nose scrunches at the sight of the garment, an eyesore in such an already boring room. The scythe, however, has a unique appeal to it. It reflects the soft red light of the time clock, and it has a frequency that pulls Opal to it. While it was on her back, the weight was not like the weight that pulls you under an ocean wave, but that of a warm hug instead.

She rises and grabs the stiff cloak. On Earth, she did not consider herself the most fashionable, but in this particular case, she couldn't wrap her head around wearing a sack of potatoes on a daily basis. There are no mirrors here, no sinks, or self-care products. She missed having a routine like brushing her teeth and taking fancy long baths.

The red countdown on the wall doesn't allow her to continue pondering her old life, alternatively snippets of the lectures of the previous day flood her mind.

"This isn't fair." She repeats to herself while throwing the cloak over her shoulders.

Three.

"I can't believe I really went through with it."

Two.

"I don't want to do this."

One.

"It's not our fault."

Her whispers echo in her small, empty room whilst she gets a looming feeling that she's being watched. On queue, the door flies open, and her feet drag as she walks to the training chamber. The walkway is overflowing with a dense gloom, with every breath and lick of her lips, a bitter taste asphyxiates her, effectively constricting her chest. But how could she feel breathless without lungs? She crosses into the training chamber, and Judas stands in the center just as usual.

"You're late." He crossed his arms, instantly regretting his tone when he caught a glimpse of her facial expression. He knew that feeling all too well.

"You're lucky I'm here at all." She bites back.

"I wouldn't call it luck–" he responds, this time a tad softer.

He decides not to wait for her answer and swings his own scythe, opening a rift. A diagonal opening, the shape of a cat's iris, jagged and slightly oval, rips across the space. Pinks and purples swirl at the edges, connecting two different dimensions at once. She surveys the resemblance of Judas's scar to the rift, only for her gaze to travel directly to his. With the soft pink and purple light bouncing off his complexion, they don't cower away this time.

"Strange." He thinks.

The mutual eye contact kept them glued to that spot until the flat side of her scythe's blade magically bent over and bonked her on the head.

"Ow!" She rubs her head. Judas laughs uncontrollably.

His non-existent abdominal muscles ached with the motion of laughing. It had been so long, he thought he wasn't capable of making that sound anymore. Despite the rules, he side glances to the right and then the left before he extends his hand towards Opal, a taboo kindness he has never granted any other Reaper. It could have been the way her shoulders sag, the way her lips are turned down, or the way she mustered a laugh out of him—he could sense the dread that tensed her shoulders and dragged her feet.

Ignorant of the rules and the nature of this interaction, Opal slides her hand on his. It was cold, and unclear how she could feel his body temperature.

"Being dead is weird. My body still feels alive." She thinks.

Judas holds tight and gently leads her through the rift; her eyes close as her knuckles turn white.

"Welcome to Medio." His hand, like a rope, not resembling the one he once bore around his neck, but rather one that holds her together.

Opal feels a rush in her head while she passes through the rift, and is immediately assaulted by the smell of sulfur overwhelming her nostrils. Microscopic particles suspended in the space dampen her eyes. The image ahead is familiar and simultaneously foreign. A distant home she might have dreamt about, with a hazy filter adding a magical blur to the scenery.

For an inconceivable second, their hands remained married once her head steadied to the environment, she released herself from his grip. He unwelcomes the sensation of their contact breaking.

The scene at her front leaves her mouth falling wide. Judas had mentioned Medio was an in-between, although she had not imagined it like this. They stood in a meadow, surrounded by tall grass and a large variety of colorful flowers. It was clearly daytime in this immutable haze. She could still hear the birds chirping and the leaves dancing to the song of the wind. Her fingertips attempted to brush a small bush of Angel's Breath; she was the breeze that toppled the white fibers off the bushel and carried them through a current of air until they landed on the ground.

"God, I miss this place. I'm on Earth and yet so far away." She fights the increasing urge to cry. "All the things I took for granted. I just wish I could understand."

"Ignorance can be bliss. Not knowing will help your transition." His hand, with a mind of its own, stretches his fingers towards her, silently reaching for her shoulder. Thinking twice, he retreats and attempts to change the subject.

"Okay," he says sharply, "I will show you how to do this Reaping thing." She embraces his change in tone and rewards him with a fracture of a smile.

He takes a moment to teach her how to cut her tie to the sustenance of the realms, giving her the ability to hover. During this interaction her scythe is just as heavy, although still comforting.

The lecture is cut short when an older lady walks through the meadow. Wrinkles adorn her face with deeply engraved smile lines.

She has a limp to her step and a small hump at the nape of her neck. Her head hangs forward as if the weight of her mind was too heavy a burden. The lady sits under the biggest Willow tree. Vibrant branches of green create a shaded area for her to rest.

Opal moves towards the tree and notices a thin glowing cord tethering the lady's chest to the ground, its light not steady but blinking. The thick Willow trunk, filled with marks collected through time, had a very specific engraving: the names Jason and Grace encircled by a heart shape. The woman was out of breath as she rested her hand on her chest while small beads of sweat ran down her temple.

"I'll see you soon, my sweet Jason." Her sweet, aged voice dimmed, and the light of her cord followed. Her chest rose and fell one last time before a serene slumber succumbed to her, leaving her body cold against that Willow tree.

Too much, this was too much for Opal. So many mixed emotions stormed inside her. "This is what it's supposed to be," she sobs, "no Rogues, peaceful, beautiful, and a full life."

A sharp SNAP! Brings her head back to why she was there in the first place, her new purpose. Judas had cut her tie to Earth, followed by a rift. He holds the end of the once luminescent rope and guides Grace to Cielo.

"How can you be so fucking brazen!" Her voice screeches.

"Opal–listen to me," he rushes to her and plants his hands on her shoulders, "there is also beauty in Death. These are the scenarios I enjoy watching. The scenario many of us wish we had." His eyes rest on Grace's lifeless body, eternally sleeping under the shade of the Willow branches.

"I'm not brazen, I'm used to it." He continues, "Our job isn't easy. Death is a natural process of life, and it is a rare occasion when someone gets to sleep forever in peace. I bet her life was as beautiful as her death." He recognizes he is still holding Opal in place, firmly holding her shoulders. He lets go and takes a few steps back. "What were you thinking?" He thinks.

"Beauty in death, huh? I don't think I have ever thought of it like that." She says, turning around to admire the picture ahead of her in a different light: a portrait of beauty and heartbreak all at once.

With one last glance, she makes her peace and waits for Judas to take them to their next destination. Upon turning around, facing him, his hand was already extended and waiting. Together they travel, one rift after another. Judas cuts ties, and she watches. Each time he ensures to hold her hand to comfort her. He did notice that her grip on his loosened after each death.

"How do you know where to go next?" Opal asks.

"The scythe is sentient. It knows the next destination and leads its wielder without hesitation. We must be prepared to face all kinds of situations." He lectures.

Reapers learn to turn a blind eye and simply perform their duty. That is the job of the Reaper, and that is the weight of their sentence.

At the end of their work day, Judas's scythe takes them to Opal's training room. She lets go of him, barely glancing back at him while retiring to her room.

He watches her, he knows she's a time bomb, he can sense it. For better or for worse, he was already invested. She has elicited so many thoughts in him in a short time. She thawed his numbness and ignited discontent for the system. Powerless, that is how he felt all this time. With Opal in the picture, he was curious that he might be wrong.

She arrives at her room. She rests her scythe on the wall and removes her cloak. Her clothes magically transform back into linen. Sitting on the wooden bench, she rests her forehead on the stone wall. Softly banging her forehead on it.

"I don't think I can do this." She says.

After she is finally able to tuck herself in, once again, the feeling of someone's eyes on the back of her head returns, but when she turns to see, there is only the opposite wall.

CHAPTER 6

Judas taps his foot while waiting for Opal in the training room. Today she is taking longer than the previous day. He opted to stand on the ground rather than hovering, she preferred to walk as much as possible, and he wanted to accommodate what he could, considering this was their last day together. After today, she will be Reaping independently without the possibility of contact with others.

"At this rate, she is bound to serve as a Reaper for all eternity. Defying the Gods never ends well." He thought.

His scythe vibrates on his back,

"I know she's coming, I can feel her. Also, could you be more helpful today?" Judas said to his scythe.

The previous day, his weapon kept taking him to perfect scenarios. He was hoping to help her cope with the more common deaths and her first encounter with Rogues. It seems his weapon might know something he doesn't.

The familiar pull in his chest tightens when he sees her approach through the door. Her undereyes are starting to form bags, and her features begin to show the drawn nature all Reapers share. The cloak is ill-fitting on her petite stature, making her look small and fragile; he knows she is far from that. On the day of her judgment nullification, she still held her head high, now her chin tucks into her neck, and her gaze roams the floors instead of the ceiling.

"Hang in there, Opal." He thought. But, hang on to what?

There was no hope for either of them. They were condemned. They held no true power against the rulers of this realm. He wondered if maybe there was some place to run away. He couldn't do it anyway. His soul was already heavy from guilt, running away from a punishment he felt he deserved felt wrong. However, helping her run away, if the time ever came for that, might be something he might be able to do.

"Ready?" He asks, avoiding the urge to reproach her for her tardiness, not when he doesn't know what her scythe will show her today. He tries softening his posture while noting how unusually quiet she is today.

"Opal?"

"I–I don't want to do this." A weak sob escapes her full lips.

She avoids eye contact and wallows in self-pity. She wasn't able to sleep. She attempted to rest on the bench in her room, tossing and turning. Through her insomnia, she was able to catch a glimpse of the time the red clock starts, turns out it's twenty minutes.

Judas stands waiting for her to ready herself, another act of kindness he hasn't offered anyone else. Her presence in itself made him want to break all rules just to make a smile return. To him, she was both an unbendable metal and a fragile glass, like a grenade he wasn't sure how to handle or what the outcome would be if she broke.

"You're standing." She states the obvious.

"Yeah…about that. I'm trying to get used to walking again."

"Has being dead made you into a toddler or something?" She retorts.

"No, it's just that hovering is a lot easier, and you get used to it." His smile is followed by her loud sigh.

For the first time, Opal reaches for her hood and covers her face, just like she did on Earth with her smile. She could pretend to be a Reaper. She could also pretend to be good at it. For how long? Was the real question. The heaviness of her scythe in her hands tugged at her shoulders when she swung the beak of the blade, and fractured the world towards the official start of her sentence. She allows herself to hover, and this time she offers her hand to Judas. He takes it without hesitation and hovers through the portal behind her, effectively letting her take the lead.

They arrive on the hazy version of Earth: the Medio dimension. They landed somewhere in a hospital, with white walls and healthcare staff running around in different colored scrubs. Alarm sounds are muffled, but the chaos stirred in the hallway is evident as nurses, aids, and other specialties run towards a specific room. This environment was something Opal was familiar with. She doesn't remember how she took her own life, but she does remember who she was. She was a nursing assistant, and some of her last memories were of a hospital during a global pandemic. She wondered if that was still going on.

As they hover towards the room with all of the commotion, a few employees shiver with their breeze: death knocking on the door. A full resuscitation attempt was being performed on a patient, although the look on the staff's face indicated their efforts were hopeless. The patient is a larger man. He was already intubated, and the respiratory technician was already bagging him. The chest compressions were deep, and the sound of his ribs cracking resounded through the space. A line of compressors was formed behind the current one, waiting for their turn and ready to take their place. The doctor stood at the foot of the bed, giving orders and assessing the situation.

A chill runs down her spine when she spots them. Dark entities are hovering over each person in the room. A small Rogue, like an elf on a shelf, with pointy red horns, multiplying and poking every person's stomach. Uncertainty resembles small, black, floating orbs with a single mouth whispering in the ears of anyone who would listen.

"You didn't do enough." It whispers into the doctor's ears.

"How long has this been going on? She asks Judas.

"There is no way of knowing exactly how long, but your scythe brought us here, so he must be close." He stands behind her, gauging her reaction to the chaos and the Rogues. He was having a hard time reading her, though, with her hood on, and he couldn't see her face.

At that very moment, the patient's wife was brought into the room, and she knew what this meant. There was nothing to do, and the family was likely refusing to put a stop to the resuscitation attempts. They couldn't even shock him anymore; there was no electrical activity in his heart. He was technically dead already. The string tethered to his chest had already stopped glowing, but she wasn't going to take his soul until his wife said so.

"Marianne, our efforts have been going on for about twenty minutes, and he has not responded to anything. We believe that it's time to stop CPR." The case manager says to her.

In that moment, Opal saw the Rogue following Marianne: Grief. It's a seven-foot-tall, pitch-black Rogue, with no facial features or horns, but it has two muscular and enormous arms that slightly drag behind it on the ground. A fist is airborne, and it lands right on Marianne's chest. The team is still performing chest compressions as she watches what nightmares are made of. Again and again and again.

Opal's hand tightens on her scythe, sensing that Judas was watching her every move and the fact that she should have cut his cord a while ago. For whatever reason, Judas thought it was important for her to witness the whole scene, yet another broken rule. Opal knew what it was like to participate in those situations. She remembers feeling those Rogues and the pain they inflict. Another five minutes pass. And Marianne is now infested.

Sadness, an indigo Rogue draped around her shoulders, shaped like a hairless sloth. Its arms tightly hold Marianne's neck like a bamboo branch, creating the feeling of a knot in her throat. Denial and Rage continue the torture alongside Grief and sadness.

"Enough! I agree. Stop his suffering." Marianne says.

When the doctors give the order to stop resuscitation efforts, Opal readies her scythe. The blade cuts through it. The cord was springy, like fishing wire.

"Time of death 22:03." The doctor announces.

Although her husband's suffering stopped, hers prevailed when Grief lifts both its arms up, folding its hands into a fist, bigger than its own head. His fist drops down onto Marianne's chest with its full weight, enough to buckle her knees straight onto the ground. The staff around her help escort her out as her Rogues follow close behind, pushing and poking at her with one motive. Opal could only hope that she had family to comfort her and help keep those Rogues at bay.

The room is still infested, and she can no longer bear it. She holds the end of the rope, a thin feather in her fingertips, and escorts the man's soul to Cielo. She doesn't look back at the aftermath of the scene when she opens another jagged rift to the next Reaping.

The following deaths were just as traumatic, but all of natural causes, like sickness and old age. Her scythe provides respite after the initial death. Judas follows behind her, uneasy about her. He senses turmoil brewing in her as she calmly Reaps, hiding under her hood. He understood her a little more this time. She is having an internal battle against her moral compass.

"Are we really powerless?" He thinks.

He admired her opening the next rift that took them back to the training room, where her hood stayed up.

"Opal, um—you did well today." He praised gently.

She didn't bother responding, but she did muster a glance his way, not understanding that this was meant to be their goodbye. She goes to her room whilst forming a hard shell around herself, leaving no room in her fortress to acknowledge that growing feeling in her non-existent heart.

"Wait!" Judas pleads behind her, although too late.

She has already arrived in her room. Without thinking, he rushes to her door. It was forbidden for Reapers to visit each other or interact outside of the three days of training. Comradery was something the Gods wanted to avoid to prevent retaliation from the Reapers, as a result, solitude was embedded into their sentence.

He stood outside her door, a flutter in his chest making him ponder if this was worth the trouble. Pacing back and forth outside her door, trying not to fall off the small walkway, he decides on the latter. He rests his hand on her door, followed by his forehead, briefly trying to channel some courage through it. In this moment, he unintentionally vowed to help her in any way he could when the time came.

The scythe on his back vibrates as it had never before.

"Do what you must, Opal. Something tells me that this will not be the last time I see you." He whispered more in reassurance to himself than for her to hear.

CHAPTER 7

Opal awakens and immediately starts her morning routine. Every day, she wakes before the red clock begins its countdown, giving her time to prepare, providing a semblance of normalcy. She stretches and exercises in her room because even if corporal pains were part of her sentence, weakness was not. It has been a full year since she parted ways with Judas on that last day of training. Throughout this time, she has become more conditioned and toned, and wielding her scythe is easier with her newfound strength.

She hasn't had any actual confrontations with Rogues, but she has witnessed how massive some of them can get. From the sidelines, she observed how effective they were at tormenting souls. Her hood gave her comfort and made her feel safe. Opal kept her eyes trained on the ground while she fought to keep the flashbacks of how she experienced them at bay.

In addition to her physical preparation, she incorporated scythe practice into her routine, perfecting the Third and Fourth movements. This morning, Opal attempted to combine movements. She practiced transitioning between the two, and she also began creating her own. She savored the idea of her blade's sharp edge cutting through those damned monsters. Besides, Judas had only said not to play around with her scythe. He never mentioned anything about creating new movements.

Occasionally, especially during her training session, Judas's face appeared in her mind, guilt poking at her for not saying goodbye or thanking him the last time they saw each other. Sometimes, when she was having trouble sleeping, she would imagine the subtle way his brow scrunched when he looked at her, or the way his calloused hands held her own those counted times, which helped her soothe into sleep whilst an ache formed in her chest. Every time she thought of him, she longed to see him again, but that would never happen. They will never see each other again. That was their fate, just like many aspects of her afterlife, she didn't agree with this either.

With time and practice, Opal's movements are now fluid and her scythe is now an extension of herself. She developed a codependent relationship with it after it showed some pretense of anthropomorphic behavior. In a place so lonely as this one, her weapon was the closest thing to life.

"Your name is Pearl. Do you like it?" She had said halfway through the year. The scythe vibrated in answer, and that was the start of a lovely friendship stemming from isolation. Pearl led her wherever it wanted, and Opal followed without questioning. As any friend would, she took care of her. Pearl always looked spotless, even so she would still use her cloak to wipe it down after every day.

"Ready for another day of soul farming?" She joked while her tone was cloudier than a rainy day on Earth. Pearl's base bends, landing the flat portion of the blade on Opal's head, and then going back to its erect position as if it never happened.

"Ow! I get it, you didn't like the joke." She rubs her head.

The days felt longer, and like any job on Earth, they were exhausted. She marked the wall with another tally, Opal's way of keeping time. There were no calendars in the afterlife, the only semblance of time was her tally marks, the countdown clock, and whenever Pearl opens a rift back to the Reaping room, once named the Training room during the time Judas was still in the picture, signaling the day is over. Together, they followed a routine that, after a year, turned repetitive.

This day, just like the rest, her hood stays on. A gesture that makes the job manageable. Every day, the feeling that someone observes her grows increasingly unsettling. She assumes it's Pearl's sentience and brushes it off. She walks to the boring, round Reaping room. The chalkboard is still tucked in the corner where she placed it the first day without Judas, it still had his drawings on it. Opal enjoyed looking at it, like one would a painting at a museum.

The Reaping room is the single space connected to her room. She refused to open rifts in her resting place. She didn't want the stench of death to adorn her only personal space.

"Alright, let's go." She swings Pearl diagonally and rips a rift, quickly jumping through.

CHAPTER 8

The following day, the same routine is repeated. Opal wakes up, she performs her sit-ups, push-ups, she uses the small ledge above the door to do pull-ups, a few sets of jumping jacks, and ends her exercise routine with wall sits. After throwing her cloak on, Opal heads to the Reaping room and wields Pearl, practicing the new movement she invented. She can feel her body strengthening and her skills improving.

The energy in the room feels distinct today. The world is always quiet now, but today it's static. She holds her friend in one hand, as she's about to pull her hood over her head, when she is interrupted by Pearl's violent vibrations. Without ceasing, her blade points and bends forward.

"Whoa! Girly? What's going on?" The vibrations only intensify.

"What are you trying to tell me? What's the hurry?" She asks.

Her scythe is begging to be swung, and she does not intend to keep her waiting any longer. Something leers behind her when she hastily opens a rift. Even the swirls around the edges of the opening move rapidly, rushing her to walk through. Goosebumps rise on her skin when she feels eyes on her back again, but Pearl's intensified vibration brings her attention back.

"What in the hell?" She says.

Opal is home. The familiarity of the two-story house and the hazy nature of the realm, like an old painting. Pearl continues to tremble steadily. She somehow landed in her old room, strolling through, and she noticed how everything was exactly how she had left it. But, her bed looked slept in, next to it was her mother's alarm clock and prayer book sitting on the nightstand. She runs her hand through the mattress.

"I'm so sorry momma..." she says, "Pearl, why are we here?"

She wanders her pretty pink room, adorned with flowers painted on the walls. Her mother and father had always gone out of their way to customize each of their rooms. They both tried making their house feel like a home, and their mother had a detail-oriented nature. She personally painted her siblings' and her own room. Opal's was pink and green with flowers, Redeam's room was purple with a decorative purple trim, and Rubin's room was light blue with little red cars sporadically adorning the walls. Opal was very close to her siblings, even with the youngest, who was eight years younger. But, before Rubin came into the picture, Opal and Redeam were two peas in a pod. They shared and fought over everything, and their love was unconditional.

She exited her room, and the corridor from the second floor was desolate. Across from her room was Redeam's, a dim light shines from underneath the door. Her hand lands on the doorknob, twisting the door open. Redeem is three years older than her, and her room was slightly bigger in comparison.

"Hello? Is anyone home?" She asks out loud, well aware that even if someone was home, they wouldn't be able to hear her.

With a loud creek and Pearl violently quaking again, Opal follows that dim light inside the room. There she is, the most grand person she knows, looking smaller than ever. The cord on her chest is tightly tethered and still glowing bright.

"Pearl?" She asks for clarification, but in her gut she knows exactly what's going on. She stands, eyes wide, comparable to a deer in headlights.

To Opal, Redeam was the strongest and happiest of people. She danced around and joked with everyone. Her heart was enormous and full of life. There was no task too big or impossible for her. However, there was one task she found difficult to do, that is living without her sister.

In her hand rests a small doll. A blonde fairy with a pink rose petal dress and green vines as shoes. The doll's face was covered in droplets raining from Redeam's eyes.

"I remember her! That's my favorite doll from the movie Fairies and Topia." Excitement fluttered in Opal's chest for a fracture of a moment until the truth fully hit her.

"Oh, Redeam, no–don't do this." She whispers.

Inch by inch, she approaches her sister; the shadows afflicting and the small, sharp knife tight in her other hand. She is surrounded by her own hoard of Rogues, all stilling while death hovers close. Without hesitation, her hand caresses her sister's cheek; she is the delicate current of wind gently swaying Redeam's hair off her face.

Depression, Anxiety, Hopelessness, Grief, and Guilt growl at the interaction and her breach of the rules. In that moment, she couldn't bother paying attention to the Rogues, not when there was a folded letter labeled "Familia." Opal grabs the letter: an air current topples it open. Redeam too deep into her mental state to even notice.

Dear Mom, Dad, and Little Rubin,

    I write this letter to tell you, I'm sorry for doing this to you again. Life is not worth living without my Opal, and I intend to follow her and meet up with her wherever she is. I know you guys wouldn't want her to be alone. Maybe if I were nicer to her, or if I cared for her better, she might still be here. It should have been me. I will not let her spend her time in heaven alone. I love, and I promise I will say hi to her for you.

    - With Love Redeam

"You can't do this! I don't want this for you!" She pleads with her hands on her shoulders, shaking her awake; a strong current of air vigorously sways her back and forth. It doesn't work. She still has a glassy nature to her eyes.

Depression, a six-foot-tall Rogue, its body resembling that of a lumberjack, completely black and devoid of features, with an up-side-down crescent moon of a head and two hammerhead-shaped fists. It stands. It does not wait for any further interactions. Its bulky semblance towers over both of them when he slams its enormous hammer fists into her chest. Taking turns with Grief, pounding into Redeam's sternum.

Anxiety, with its lightning strike figure, is flexible and twig-like. An eyeball sits on every sharp corner of its body, its branches poke at Redeam's arms and legs, sending currents of panic to coarse through her veins. Hopelessness, a black raven carrying grand black wings and missing its core. It has a hole in the center of its body, and the head is composed of a large beak and two red beaded eyes. With its beak, it endlessly pokes at her head, like small, raining pebbles, over and over: a never-ending hail storm.

Stomp...Stomp...Stomp...

The realm trembles when Guilt approaches, ominous and enormous. Towering high above Opal and Redeam, this whole time it stood at the sidelines, hidden within the shadows. About eleven feet tall, a bald, husky man, with an icy hue to its arms and legs.

Opal steps away from her sister, watching as those things consume her soul, how they poke and prod at her, how they whisper in her ears. And how Guilt shook her with each stomp of its feet. She remembered what it felt like to have Guilt glooming in the sidelines while she was alive.

A sudden onset of dizziness, the world spins for Opal, and sharp flashbacks of a bathtub, a blood clot, and hot water. When something SNAPS!

It's not Redeam's time to Earth, while her hand swiftly picks up the sharp fruit knife, likely stolen from the kitchen downstairs. But it was Opal's scythe moving freely at her fingertips. Her cloak sways around her as she fans the blade into a sharp windmill.

Time stops when her deadly fan makes contact with Anxiety and Hopelessness.

"Get off my sister, assholes!"

Anxiety and Hopelessness are gone, and with that alone, Redeam stops cutting into her wrists. One single drop of blood stains her skin. She stills in the center of her bed as if she were a statue standing in the middle of a fight for her life. Depression continues hammering her chest, and Grief turns its attention towards Opal. Guilt, still stomping the ground, shaking the realm, not satisfied, it slams its fists into the ground, sending cracks towards Redeam. The cracks on the floor that race towards her get wider as they approach her.

Pearl is spun from one hand to another. There isn't much time. The beak of the blade draws a cross in the air: Third movement. Guilt is frozen in place, and so are the cracks on the ground. It viciously growls, fighting the hold. Like Judas, her movements were second nature to Opal. She repeats the fanning motion of the Fourth movement, like the one she used to kill Anxiety and Hopelessness. Grief is sent into flying pieces of coal, black dust covers the air, leaving her to look like a chimney sweep. Depression pauses its attack on Redeam, halting and slowly retreating.

She scowls at Guilt, frozen before her. How the tides have turned, she didn't care how long it would be frozen for. This was the opportunity she was waiting for.

"I've been meaning to settle shit with you, this little gift is called—" she thinks for a split second about the redundancy of the situation. She was once the one crippled with Guilt, and now it was crippled by her, "Cycle of life." She finishes.

Holding the bottom of Pearl's base, she leverages herself back, letting the weight of her scythe move around her as she becomes the eye of the storm. She spins, picking up speed, faster, and faster. She has become a vengeful tornado, a vortex of pure speed and momentum, gradually levitating into the air with the force of her speed. The storm plunges forward, landing her blade on Guilt's musty bald head. It's eviscerated and blown into black sandy rain, and the cracks on the ground healed. She turns to give Depression the hell it deserves, but the coward has run away.

On the bed, Redeam's clear consciousness awakens, and her glassy eyes unveil.

"Oh God, oh God," Redeam says, throwing the knife across the bed. She grabs the letter and tears it into a thousand pieces. With the doll still in her hand, she inspects the room, and for the briefest of moments, Opal swears their eyes met.

"Thank you, baby sis. I know it was you." She says, while Opal embraces her. A gentle current comforts her in a cool hug. Tears slide down the slopes of their cheeks, both a mirror of each other.

The moment is interrupted by the heavenly horn, similar to the one that wails when it's time to wake up, but much louder. The largest rift Opal has ever seen opens behind her. The Gods found out about her actions, and she knew her prosecution was inevitable. She kisses her sister's temple goodbye. Opal mounts Pearl on her back.

"Thank you, Pearl, for bringing me here." She says. Pearl's blade bends at the base, and with the flat side, it doesn't hit her head as she usually does, but gently pats her instead.

This was the prime example, not only because it was her sister but because Redeam showed that she didn't want to take her life and that the influence of the Rogues is too heavy a burden. Her head is high as she walks through the rift, this time ready to defy the Gods without an ounce of remorse. Without noticing, for the first time in a year, her hood was completely off.

CHAPTER 9

"Do you have any idea what you've done!" Deus's loud voice welcomes Opal's return to the judgment chamber.

The tall three sit in their respective thrones. In the gold throne sat its corresponding golden God, Deus. He owns the physique of a bodybuilder, with rippling corded muscle in full display under a barely there tunic, side-swept on one of his shoulders. His golden blonde hair, middle parted in small waves, perfectly frames his square-shaped face. Green piercing eyes, with a cold expression and disgust as he looks at Opal. Behind his rough nature stood a grand, although delicate golden wing, with feathers larger than Opal herself.

In the center, the white throne sat the most beautiful woman she had ever seen, Parity. She is the embodiment of statuesque grace. As if she's made of marble, pure white with only a sheer blush on her cheeks and lips. She wears a dress made of the finest chiffon. Or could it be silk? Did those materials exist in this realm? Effortlessly draping off her shoulders, from Opal's distance, it almost looked wet. Her white hair was set into an elegant messy side bun, and a glimmering halo framed her head.

To the right of her, in the dark silver throne, sat Dannato. A haunting beauty adorned in black, intricate armor. His wide shoulders are framed by a beautiful, flowing cape, and on his head sat a six-pointed crown with red jewels. His hair is long, jet black, and sleek, in high contrast with his pale complexion. His eyes, the same color as the red apple he held in his hand, pierced through Opal like a spear.

Opal stands on the podium at the center of the chamber for the second time. Pearl pulls her posture straight, helping her keep her chin up. She openly stares at them, now that they are in full display, she can admire them until she realizes they all scowl at her in disapproval. After Deus's outburst, silence filled the chamber until Dannato broke the tension with the sound of a crunch from his apple.

"Child, recite the law of the Reaper." Parity commands with her delicate poise.

"The law of the Reaper is that we don't interfere," Opal says through her teeth.

"What is that again?" She says, clearly not satisfied with the way Opal broadcasted.

"The Law...of the Reaper...is that...we...don't interfere," Opal says, elongating every few words as if she were talking to a child. The Gods did not sympathize with her current tone; in fact, they felt ridiculed. With a snap of his finger, Dannato briefly transported Opal to the Underworld.

Torment, gore, suffering. Souls in agony. The punishments he deemed fit for those who were condemned, she saw her future. Boiling cauldrons filled to the brim with people, chambers in flames engulfing humans limb by limb, and their screams. Oh, the screams and the wails in pain shatter through her non-existent eardrums. The smell of burning flesh and charred hair roasts her nose hairs. And, her soul felt vacuumed into the never-ending darkness that was this pocket of the Underworld. Another snap of his fingers, and she was back in the chamber behind the safety of her podium.

"Think again how you address us," Dannato says.

"Is that what the Underworld is like for everyone?"

"Not everyone. Only if I think you deserve it. Now, please recite the law *correctly*." His red eyes glow, a cat ready to pounce on a midnight snack.

This time, Opal recites the law in a perfectly respectful tone of voice, still keeping her head high. Trying to fight off the shivers that place elicited in her.

"Are you saying you broke the law on purpose?" Dannato taunts.

Opal knew her actions would have consequences. But one thing she wasn't going to accept was to be judged without being heard. Since she arrived in the afterlife, the one thing she should have been entitled to was a judgment, but after it was nullified, her feelings didn't matter anymore. However, now she has a premise for a case. She decided that she didn't care if she ended up in a boiling cauldron, as long as she was heard.

"Are you saying that *you*," she points at the three of them, "are content with letting humans die at the hands of those monsters? They interfere with life and death. Why can't we? Why don't *you*?" If she had blood, it would boil.

The nerve these so-called Gods had to create life and not protect it. To let outside forces play, infest, and manipulate them. She stood there waiting for answers, pleading with her eyes to each of them. Dannato caught it, her silent plea.

Of the three Gods, he actually pondered the question. Taken aback by her confrontation and her lack of cower, but somewhat impressed at her courage to do so, even after seeing her possible future.

"You dare question us?!" The golden God's voice is loud and apparently the only volume he knows how to use.

"She has a point." Dannato retorts, seemingly amused by this whole interaction.

"She broke Divine Law! She interfered out of selfishness, which has nothing to do with us. Human life sprouted from our creation, and we rule as we see fit." Deus shouts, while Dannato cups his ears with his hands, all while rolling his eyes.

"Say she broke the rules, but I disagree. She did it out of love for her sister. No one inherently evil would put their eternity at risk for someone they love." Parity says while she sits up straight with perfect posture.

"My eternity? At risk? I'm already going to hell! Besides, is Redeam not the perfect example of how Rogues force humans to commit suicide? After I interfered, she didn't want to do it at all. That should have meant something." Opal stands her ground.

The Gods send each other a weary look. The God of the Underworld raises his brow at her outrage. Amongst the three of them, they begin to argue.

"It is possible we might have let the Rogues get too far? It might be time we consider intervention for the sake of balance." Parity adds.

"There is balance. This human only wants a better outcome for herself." The golden angel says.

"If that was the case, she wouldn't have the guts to talk to us in that manner after I showed her what the possible consequences would be. I agree with Parity, this matter requires our attention." Dannato raises.

With each argument becoming more divisive, Opal stood listening to their pitches, all while being ignored, and in the meantime, millions of people were persuaded to forfeit their lives.

"No human has ever defied our laws!" Deus shouts across the chamber.

"There was never a need, or maybe there was, and we just didn't realize it. Maybe—we are so complacent in our respective roles that we never considered that our law is indeed not fair." Dannato bites his apple. "You are too busy sitting in your perfect cloud of grace surrounded by all your cherubs. Parity is teaching humans lessons in the afterlife, and I monitor the Underworld to ensure fairness amongst punishments. What if, in the case of Reapers, we have not been entirely just? " He finishes, now scratching his jaw, lost in thought.

While Deus and Dannato went at each other's throats, Parity elegantly studied Opal. She watched her stand tall at the podium and patiently wait for the verdict. The God of Purgatory tapped her finger on the arm of the white throne when Deus stood abruptly.

"Enough!" She scolds both of them but signals Deus to sit. After her eyes soften, he decides to listen and sits with his arms crossed.

"The bottom line is that she can not continue Reaping until a decision is made about the proceedings of this situation. We may have to consider an accommodation while we come to such a conclusion." She says, swiftly looking at both the Gods at her sides.

Panic rises up Opal's throat, as her thoughts run one-hundred miles per hour.

"If I can't Reap, I can't interfere. If I can't interfere, what good was this whole confrontation?" She thinks.

The time it would take the Gods to come to a decision was unprecedented, and Opal was not willing to waste so much time while she could be doing something about this. They expected her to sit still in some "accommodation" while people, like her, like Redeam, suffered at the claws of those filthy things. Not like that, not on her watch. Opal watches their discussion, waiting for it to become increasingly heated. When Pearl interrupts her train of thought, subtly vibrating on her back.

"You read my mind." She whispers to her scythe.

Inching her hand towards her back, keeping an eye on the three deities ahead, tuning out their words but simply waiting for her opening. It takes one resonating shout from Deus to mask the sound of a rift opening and Opal jumping through it. She slips into Medio for a second time, this time as a Rogue herself.

CHAPTER 10

"Holy shit! We've done it now." Opal says to Pearl while pacing from one side to the other.

She had opened and closed about a dozen rifts until she felt safe enough to stop. Her scythe led her through different pockets of the realm until they landed in this one. Turns out there is more to this dimension than she originally thought. For the moment, she stands in the center of some pocket of Medio with no souls to Reap.

"I don't know where I am. I don't really know what I've done. I don't know what to do next." Her words quiver while her scythe trembles on her back, likely just as scared as she is.

Opal stopped her frantic pacing and centered herself with a few deep breaths, but without lungs or air, no relief came from it. They stood in a void surrounded by absolutely nothing. There was no up, down, or place to sit down. Only her fears brewing in her mind made a sound, because what else could she possibly lose? Her life, Reaping, her eternity, well—maybe that's for the better. An eternity running away might be better than being tortured in one of those boiling cauldrons for the rest of time. However, that didn't matter. Opal's chest caved, heavy, as her mind wandered through the endless possibilities of her fate.

She progressed from being a lost soul on Earth to literally being a lost soul. Panic breaks a sob free from her, her actions weighing heavily on her shoulders. Or was it Pearl? Everything spun, and she felt lightheaded as the realm spun around her. She wasn't capable of breathing, and yet she couldn't catch her breath.

She avoided confrontation at all costs on Earth and never felt comfortable standing in the center of chaos. This was different. The stakes were higher and more important than her own life. Everyone was at stake. And, through those thoughts of self-degradation, bargaining, and victimization, it dawned on her; she ran away, but to what merit?

"I ran away." She sobs, finally crumbling to her knees, on what she thought might be the ground, and holds her face in her palms.

"I RAN AWAY AGAIN!" Her voice echoes through the empty space.

A place where no matter, no particles, even atoms were mythical, and somehow it was possible for her to exist in that very space. Her scythe sits on her back still shaking at a steady rate, adding the weight of a hug to her back, and bending to pat her head as it sometimes did.

"Pearl, I don't want to keep running away." Pearl stops patting her head. The flat side of her blade just sits on the top of her head, like a friend setting her chin on her head in comfort.

The image of her sister appears in her mind, the little doll she held on to, and the memories that doll represented. She pondered.

"To Redeam, holding that doll was like holding me. She didn't want to kill herself. She just wanted to see me again. Grief, Guilt, Hopelessness, are all natural feelings. Human feelings and Rogues know that. They understand their power over us and use it to their advantage." She speaks to herself and Pearl, because who else could be listening?

"We all deserve the courtesy in life that I am allowing myself at this very moment. We deserve to sit with our emotions without plaguing monsters pushing us to their will. We deserve to have someone to fight for us. We deserve a second chance. If they won't do it, then I will." She continues.

Her hood is still off, showcasing all that she is. Strong. Assertive. Brave. She wipes her tears with the back of her hand, and Pearl stands erect again.

"Hey Pearl, after I'm done having my afterlife crisis, would you like to join me in my noble crusade?" She smiles when her friend vibrates in agreement. Excitement grows from the despair in her chest, and the plan begins to form. Opal will interfere in as many suicides as possible before the inevitable happens: her capture.

"The inevitable." She thought.

She didn't know what was going to happen or what the Gods would do. Was there a worse fate than the Underworld? All she knows is that until that happens, she can help many. To her, everyone was worth fighting for.

She dismounts her friend from her back. They are both ready to begin a journey they are unsure they can finish, and welcome the consequences they will get for trying. She forces herself to stand just as straight as Pearl.

With the same practiced motion as before, she fractures the realm of Medio and says, "Alright, let's go."

CHAPTER 11

The task of taking on Rogues was easier thought of than executed because her knowledge of them was limited, and her experience fighting them was one encounter. Rogues were both very simple and extremely complicated creatures. She thinks of the lesson Judas gave her and remembers how little she paid attention to that part of the lesson; instead, she was focused on the sharp line of his jaw.

"Rogues have abilities that affect humans, but to Reapers, they are only able to use brute force. We do not get to have many interactions with them because, well, there is no need, so the Third and Fourth movements are enough for us to learn." Judas had said.

As a result of her limited knowledge, the first interferences were a challenge, Pearl caught on, and took Opal to more manageable Reapings.

"Oh, Judas, you were so wrong they can totally do more than use brute force." She thought while being held captive by two pairs of shadow claws from Envy. It was about a mile away, whispering bitter nothings into a teenage girl's ear.

"How come she has a loving family and you don't?" Envy said to her.

After Opal was able to dislodge herself from its claws, she swiftly turned it into cinders. The Reapings after that one were equally challenging, if not more.

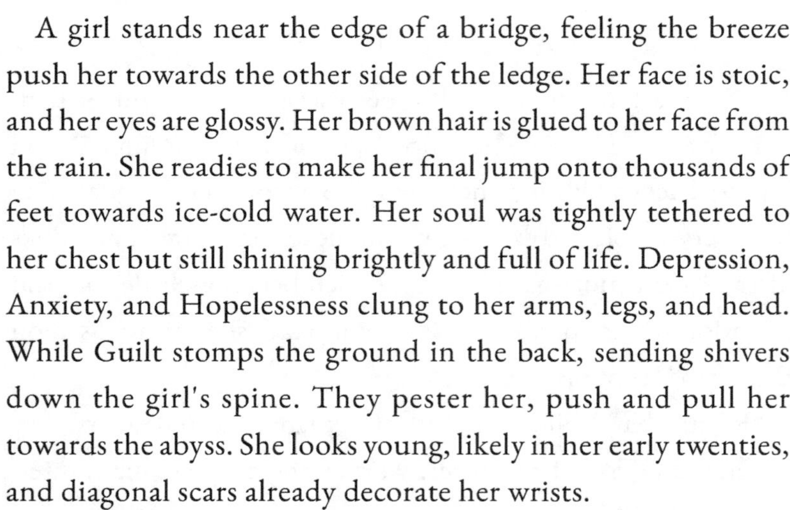

A girl stands near the edge of a bridge, feeling the breeze push her towards the other side of the ledge. Her face is stoic, and her eyes are glossy. Her brown hair is glued to her face from the rain. She readies to make her final jump onto thousands of feet towards ice-cold water. Her soul was tightly tethered to her chest but still shining brightly and full of life. Depression, Anxiety, and Hopelessness clung to her arms, legs, and head. While Guilt stomps the ground in the back, sending shivers down the girl's spine. They pester her, push and pull her towards the abyss. She looks young, likely in her early twenties, and diagonal scars already decorate her wrists.

"You're useless."

"You're the fuck up of the family. They won't even miss you."

"No one will notice you're dead!"

"Jump, Abigail. Jump...Jump...JUMP!"

One by one, Opal peeled them off her, like a self-adhering bandage. Pearl slashed in all different directions. Third movement. Fourth Movement. Cycle of life. She was mastering the transitions and learning to use them together to cause the most damage as fast as possible. A dust storm of sand made of coal rained all over Abigail and Opal. She is Rogueless but still stands at the ledge of the bridge contemplating her decisions. Time wasn't on her side, but with no signs of Reapers, she risked staying a moment longer.

"Please don't do it. I know life is hard, but I promise there is someone who cares. I know there are people who love you and are waiting for you. So please, Abigail, don't do it." Opal drops to her knees and joins her hands in prayer, hoping her words, just as the Rogue's can reach her.

Who was she praying to? She knows that the Gods aren't listening, at least not these Gods. She stands and walks alongside Abigail by the ledge, and does the only thing she could think of, a hug, a human interaction that only one of them felt entirely. But the other felt a gentle breeze toss her hair and help her off the ledge.

That was all it took. Her eyes re-awakened from that glassy coma, and she fully dismounted the ledge to safety. A bystander's car stops at the scene, and an older lady runs to Abigail. She was unaware of their possible connection, but Opal felt the job was complete. Abigail studies her hand, wondering what that feeling was, like someone was holding it this whole time.

A small boy sits on the floor in the far corner of the closet in his bedroom. He holds his mother's sleeping medications in his hand. His dad and mom are shouting in the other room as he rests his head between his knees, trying desperately to muffle the sound of glass breaking. The room reeks of vomit, feces, alcohol, and cigarette smoke. The walls are adorned with multiple stains and growing mold. There are holes punched into the drywall. His skin has multiple patches of discoloration and bruises, and towering above him is his Rogue, Loneliness, who holds his shoulders in fake camaraderie. It stands tall and slim with irregularly long arms and legs, with long, sharp claws and talons. Its head is quite small in comparison to its protruding horns; similarly to so many Rogues, it's pitch black like a shadow in a lucid dream, whispering into his ears.

"Drink them, and the darkness won't scare you any longer."

"They don't protect you, but I will, if you drink them."

"I know they don't play with you, but I will, if you drink them."

"Drink them, Mikey, DRINK THEM!"

The sticky voice from loneliness makes Opal's skin crawl, as one would in the presence of an old nemesis. She stands listening to loads of spiteful words, it says to the boy, the same words she slightly remembers hearing too.

"Enough!" She demands, "This stops now."

"The Rogue Reaper isn't it?" Loneliness now directs its venom at her. Its claws are still deeply rooted in the boy's shoulders.

"You don't remember me, Opal? We used to be well acquainted." It says through a grin.

"Your words don't affect me anymore." She tightens her grip on Pearl when her scythe begins to vibrate in caution.

Third movement, her blade slices a cross through the space. Loneliness is paralyzed, but continues whispering through its sealed lips.

"Come on, Mikey, drink them. Don't you want all of that noise to stop? Aren't you tired of them fighting over you?" It says.

"Don't you get it, you're alone because nobody wants you."

"You're alone because you're not worthy of anyone's time."

"Drink them, they can't wait to get rid of you."

"Drink them, you're worthy of my time." It continues.

"Oh shut the hell up." She walks towards Loneliness and with the base of Pearl, she swings like a bat and homeruns its head clean off his shoulders. But even as he stands decapitated, it hums a sinister tune, like she's running out of time.

Fourth movement, Pearl is spun into that usual deadly fan in the direction of the headless body holding the boy captive. Mikey struggles to open the child-safe pill bottle, buying her some time. She hits it with a blow, a blow that usually ends in black rain. This time, its top half is still held up and defying gravity.

As she is about to attempt the fourth movement again, a bright light of purples and pinks catches her attention.

"Stop right there!" A single Reaper stands behind her, his voice masculine.

"Do you think I'll let you continue breaking the law?" He says.

"I don't care what you think." She says as she fans Pearl once again and completes the job once and for all.

The situation at hand doesn't allow her to stop and show the boy that he's not alone in such a terrible situation. She stood powerless against Mikey's living conditions and only hoped someone in his life would fight for him like she did today.

The Reaper approaches Opal, scythe in hand. She braces, ready for impact and determined to fight. Maybe she could knock some sense into him. Before their blades collide, another rift opens next to the current Reaper.

"You might care what I think." Another voice, a familiar voice, one she still thinks about.

This Reaper emerges from the rift, and she immediately recognizes him, not only by his voice and the prominent scar on his neck but also by the thud that he caused in her heartless chest.

"Leave, I'll handle this." Judas commands the other. What gives him the authority to boss other Reapers around? Was it his seniority or favoritism from the Gods? Or was it something else?

"The Gods will hear about this."

"They are the ones who sent me here, go Reap your next!"

The other Reaper is left without a choice as he jumps through a rift onto his next case.

"How come you get to boss others around?" Opal asks Judas, fighting the urge to run and give him the tightest hug imaginable.

"I've been around for a long time, and as such, the Gods have a soft spot for me and have given me the opportunity to hunt down a certain Rogue Reaper." He says with a wink.

"Why are you helping me?" She asks him.

"I've been thinking about all you have said, and I still don't know how I feel about all of this." He said. "How I feel about you." He thought to himself.

"So, I'll help you buy some time. I can't do it forever, but I'll do what I can." Judas says.

"Thank you, Judas. Not just for this but for before. I didn't get to say that the last time I saw you." She approaches him and gives him a small peck on his cheek. His eyes go wide at the interaction.

"Don't mention it." He responds, palming his cheek in his hand, trying to keep that kiss there forever.

Opal glances back at Mikey, who is putting the pill box away. Loneliness might be gone, but it will not take long for this boy to be plagued by Rogues again. She contemplates his heartbreaking case, opens a rift, and jumps through it.

Judas watches her jump and can't help the relief he feels from seeing her again.

—◆O◆—

One interference after another goes by, and so on. After what seemed like endless cases, Opal begins to struggle physically and emotionally. She aches all over, and that constant feeling of being observed, like a fish in a tank, is starting to give her the creeps. Although she assumed it was the Gods watching, it puzzled her how they could do that and still not capture her. Since the dimension of Medio was out of their reign, there was a chance that they had no real power here aside from opening enormous rifts. At worst, their power might be limited there. With that assumption, she kept brushing off the feeling.

"Maybe they aren't all-powerful." She converses with Pearl, never expecting an answer in return, but the occasional vibration or pat on the head is always welcomed. As a team, they came up with a warning system while interfering. Pearl only vibrates when she senses a Reaper approaching in order to avoid confusion; the scythe otherwise lets her wielder do her job.

Together, they have become a force to be reckoned with. The work was endless, and the only place to rest was the void they found at the beginning. She assumed her Reaper quarter was heavily monitored, and Pearl knew better than to take her there.

As they continue interfering, they notice Rogue's are becoming harder to defeat. Word of the Rogue Reaper has spread across the realm, making her one advantage of surprise attacks useless. She continues fighting and saving as many lives as possible. Pride and hope grew in her every time a person changed their mind, and it fueled her to keep going.

A new mother leaves her newborn baby with grandma to watch over, while she takes some personal time for self-care. She hasn't felt like herself since the delivery and has been having trouble adjusting to her body and her new life. With the new challenges of motherhood, the voices whispering in her ears, and the constant comments from her husband, she doesn't have a moment to rest.

She sits on the toilet seat waiting for the shower to warm up while thinking through everything. She thinks about how much she loves her baby and how little she loves herself, especially this new version. She stands and approaches the mirror where she analyzes her naked body and all of its flaws. The deep ridges of stretch marks, and her dark under eyes stare back at her. Her thinning hair and enlarged breasts hurt to look at. Everything hurts: her body, her mind, and her soul. In that mirror, she sees a person she does not recognize, someone her husband can't wait to get rid of.

Her hand moves to her phone, and she starts to filter through the messages her husband sends her. The bathroom is now full of steam, making it harder for her to breathe while reading his messages.

"So, how long until you hit the gym, honey?"

"I can't wait until you get your tight ass back."

"You've changed so much, Denise. Can you put a little more effort into yourself? It's hard to look at you."

"You really need to stop eating so much. My boss's wife got right back in shape after their first kid. I'll ask him to send her info, I'm sure you can get some tips on how to get rid of those huge stretch marks, and your saggy belly."

He doesn't ask about her state of mind, how she feels, or her well-being. He only cares about how she will be of use to him. She would much rather be invisible in her own home and put an end to this once and for all. In that very second, she gets a message from her husband, it's a picture from their wedding night.

"See, honey, you looked so much better here." The image shows her in her wedding dress. At that time, she wasn't aware of this side of her husband.

The hammer fists of Depression, as per usual, don't waste time. On this occasion, it is the leading Rogue of the hoard: Anxiety, Guilt, Uncertainty, Insecurity, and Body-Dysmorphia, which was new to Opal. It was similar to the rest in shade, and it had a rounded shape with a circular face with two horns, one intact and one broken in half. Body-Dysmorphia held its stomach, and when it did that, Denise mimicked its motions.

"Those stretchmarks are getting wider and uglier every day."

"You're a cow!"

It said with its deep voice.

Insecurity is flat as a piece of paper and long. It looks like a large floating banner, moving as if there was wind in the Medio realm. It has a mouth with sharp teeth protruding forward.

They all latch on to her like leeches sucking the light out of her. Poking, prodding, pushing, and pulling her towards the direction of her husband's nightstand. The bathroom adjacent to the master bedroom would make it so easy for her to get away with this. Her feet move as if in their own accord as the Rogues keep pushing, and pushing, and pushing. She opens the drawer, and inside stands a single handgun.

"Pull the trigger, Denise, pull it!"

"How can you call yourself a mother?"

"They'll be better without you, pull it! Do it! Do it!"

"You're a cow!"

"Pull it, pull it, pull it."

"You're disgusting."

"Do it, Denise. What are you waiting for?"

The hoard says in her direction, all talking at the same time, working together to get that outcome they long for.

Opal arrives with Pearl in hand, flying towards her, straight through a rift. Her curved blade lands on Guilt's enormous back, and she rides it down to the ground, leaving a gaping hole on Guilt, seconds later it rains black. She moves her scythe in the shape of a cross, Third movement. They all freeze. She throws Pearl similar to a boomerang, she hadn't named that movement yet, and in the spur of the moment, she didn't get a chance. While Pearl soared through the air, cutting through Anxiety, Body-Dysmorphia, and Helplessness, Opal ran to Insecurity, speeding up into a jump. She hovers through the space to the top of Insecurities thin banner-like figure, and tears it in half, resembling a piece of paper. She lands on the ground just as Pearl returns to her hand.

Depression is left, and it's insistent. With its hammer fists, it pounds her back, her chest, and her abdomen. Pushing, and pushing, and pushing for her to aim the gun at her head. She charges forward towards Depression. Levitating and spinning into her favorite vortex, Cycle of Life. She is the center of the windmill, powering and steering the tornado of sharp death towards the remaining Rogue, when her blade hits home.

SNAP!

Ahead of her, Depression is intact, but there is something standing in between the two. How could she miss it? How was it possible? Another Rogue, tall with three horns and bright yellow eyes, perfectly cut in half, regenerates before her eyes. Detachment stood like a wall protecting Depression, and when Opal reaches for Pearl to continue fighting, she finds her shards scattered around her instead. Frantically, she picks up the pieces of her friend, mourning the loss.

BANG!

Denise's body goes limp when it collapses to the ground. The new mother lies in a pool of crimson, lifeless. Depression is leeching onto her, contorting and moving unnaturally. Until it laughs and says.

"I won again, Opal." The sinister laugh that escapes its mouth alongside Detachment makes her skin crawl.

And from the Mother's gunshot wound, a dark shadow begins to emerge. One limb at a time, crawling out of her head in a spider adjacent way, until it stands tall. Akin to Depression, the female counterpart, in fact, is slim with a rounded belly and stripes of lightning covering her body. Post-Partum Depression is born from the diseased mother.

"No...No...No! This wasn't supposed to happen!"

It's too late, Denise's cord is no longer bright, ready to be cut. A rift opens behind her. This was it, the inevitable had caught up to her, without Pearl, she had no ability to escape.

Opal remained on the ground, cradling her broken scythe as Denise might have cradled her baby once.

"I'm so sorry, Pearl. I didn't mean to work you so hard." She holds her scythe tight while she waits for her capture. Her eyelids closed tight, tight enough to see swirling colors in the darkness behind her eyelids. One moment passes, and nothing happens. Another moment passes, and still nothing happens.

She dares to peek through one eye, and everything stands still, as if someone pressed pause on a movie. One Reaper stands by the opened rift, one very handsome Reaper. Their eyes meet, the room has a tint of green light, and it's unrecognizable with so much light filtering through. Opal doesn't care at this point. All she cares about is the man standing in front of her and her broken friend in her arms. Judas approaches and crouches down to her while looking around. He plants his hand on her cheek.

This is the second time he has been able to track her down with the help of his own scythe. It's unbearable to him to see how much sadness she carries in her eyes, how tired she looks since the last time he saw her. And even more heartbreaking when he saw the shards of her scythe rest in her arms. Behind her was an enormous, perfectly circular rift, and unlike the ones they know it had blues and green swirling at its edges.

"Go." He says to her.

"There's nowhere to run." She replies.

He helps her up, and with his hands on her shoulder, she spins her to look behind.

"Go. I keep making excuses for you, and I am having a hard time ignoring my duty. To an extent, I sympathize with your cause, but soon I will be forced to turn you in. I'm not ready to do that, Opal. So go." He fights the tug of war in his chest. One side tells him to follow the rules and that they deserve this sentence. The other says that she's right, that not just because he deserves this means everyone who commits suicide does too.

She looks at the rift, so different from the ones she knows. On the other side of it, there is a mansion made of marble columns, and Greek architecture luring her inside.

"I don't know where I will end up or if I can return." She says.

"That doesn't matter anymore. It has to be better than what awaits you in Cielo. I'll tell the Gods you slipped away. They won't believe my excuses forever, so for now I need you to go through it." His hand doesn't hold her shoulders anymore, but one of her hands, in parallel to those first times walking through rifts. He lifts one of her hands and plants a small kiss on the back of it, and steps away.

"What's another risk? I'm already condemned," she thought. Opal looks back at Judas, while he turns away to address the cord-cutting of Denise's soul. She watches, and when he's finished, she finally faces the rift. Looking ahead, Pearl's broken edges dig into her hands. No blood comes from it, only a sharp sting as she crosses through into the unknown.

CHAPTER 12

Unlike the rest of the realm of Medio, this place has personality. It's an oasis miraculously found in a desert and brings with it a breeze that brushstrokes her face and arms with goosebumps. The cool wisp of air slightly chills the damp spot on the back of her hand. If she wasn't holding the shattered pieces of her friend against her chest, she might have been able to enjoy the moment. The place surrounding her seemed straight out of a storybook.

The mansion sits on its own little island surrounded by tranquil lilac water. An eternal sunset paints the sky with colors, bathing her in varying shades of gold and orange. The breeze ushers the scent of fresh grapes and funnels the sound of classical music into her ears: the piano, violin, and tuba, accompanied by cursive soprano notes luring Opal towards the grand entrance.

She follows the melody steadily increasing in volume whilst she approaches the source. Sky-scraping white pillars frame the circumference of the building, which is only one story tall. Only by craning her neck as far back as possible could she get a glimpse of the top of the building. The entrance holds no door, only an enormous opening inviting her inside. She slips through the entrance onto a ballroom: a single open room, ornate and debatably over-decorated. The ceilings are covered in intricate paintings, a similar rendition of the Sistine Chapel. Black and white perfectly tiled and checkered floors. Such an odd mix of Greek architecture and Renaissance aesthetic is showcased through the interior design choices of the space.

As Opal wanders through the room, she is drawn by a cozy fort held up as a work of magic in the dead center of the room. Rows of white and cream colored fabric canopy over the space, and inside sits a red velvet daybed. Next to it, a brass gramophone record player was sitting on a table, and on the opposite side–

"Is that a television?" Opal's jaw nearly hits the floor.

"It is indeed, seventy-five inches of pure entertainment." A deep, sensuous voice breaks through the music.

In the once-empty daybed, there is now a gorgeous woman, graciously draped over, nibbling on grapes.

"Wait a minute, you weren't there before."

Opal notices her grey colored skin, the same color as a cloudy sky, with long, stark-white, silky hair accentuating her high cheekbones. Nothing but mischief glimmers in her light-grey eyes as her bold red lips take their time enclosing each and every grape.

"Wasn't I?" Swiftly, like a cat, she changes position, now lying on her abdomen, fluttering her feet behind. She torments a bushel of grapes, playing with them before she feasts.

"Fine, I wasn't, but I have to admit your reaction is priceless."

"And the television is for...?" Opal responds.

"This," the lady points to the television, "is how I stay entertained. Medio is so boring. Dear, you have been entertaining."

"Okay—I have so many questions." She shakes her head, while gently setting Pearl's remains on the ground, carefully placing each piece where it belongs on a black colored tile. How she missed the comfort of her scythes' weight on her back and the vibration it gave in response to her questions. How could she ever see Judas again without her weapon? How could she keep fighting without her scythe? But most importantly, how would she survive the desolate nature of her task without her friend?

Opal stands at a safe distance, keeping her eyes trained on the pretty picture before her.

"Ask away. I have nothing better to do anyway. In fact, please do get comfortable." A simple sweep of her hand, and another slightly smaller daybed appears across from hers. Opal's worn-out cloak transforms into a comfortable cotton tunic. Considering the events of the last few days, she took the offer without reproach.

Opal's long, wavy hair flies behind her when she dives into the black velvet daybed, successfully faceplanting in the center. Her muscles sing at the contact of the soft material, and almost instantaneously, her eyes beg to be closed. She decides that rest can wait; right now, she wants answers.

"What is this place?" Her voice sounds muffled as she buries her face into the cushion, all while her index finger signals around the room.

"This is my home, specifically in a different pocket of Medio. It's completely separate from those creepy baboons and soul collectors. Why? Do you like it?" She winks.

She takes a moment to peel her face from the cushion and surveys the room. Aside from the period jumble of architecture and art, she did like it. There was a unique and elegant quality to her home, making it her own.

"Who are you?" Opal says while lying back, eerily comfortable in the presence of this new being.

"My name is Era, like time. I chose it because, it's timeless and elegant just like me." A smooth laugh escapes from her as she readjusts her silky black robe.

"Have you ever heard of Deism?" Era asks.

"Vaguely, it's a philosophy of some kind." She replies.

"Humans are so ignorant. Deism is indeed a philosophy. In simple terms, it stems from the belief that there is a Godlike figure who does not interfere with human affairs. There is no term for what I am, but if I were to describe myself, I would be the self-appointed Deismae of Medio. I am not a God of your world or realm, but I do possess some abilities."

"So you're a deity that doesn't interfere with humanity that makes up words to describe herself?" Opal pauses, trying to process all of this information.

"Precisely, I do enjoy watching your species. Your kind tends to make questionable decisions, resulting in dramatic outcomes. Highly entertaining." She plops another grape in her mouth.

"We do make interesting choices, like adding pineapple to pizza." Opal giggles at the memory of old arguments with her siblings about pizza and the sacrilegious toppings people add to it.

"I see nothing wrong with that, but bringing low-rise jeans back into style is atrocious, an Underworld worthy offense in my opinion." They both laugh at Era's remark.

"Okay, next question. If you don't meddle in human affairs, why did you help me?"

"I didn't want the season, *Rogue Reaper,* to end so quickly. It's the most entertaining thing that has happened here since the first duel between Deus and Dannato, shirtless–" Era fans her face as she grins.

"Wait, you have a crush on Deus or Dannato?"

"Dannato obviously! And, can you blame me? That sulky, sad boy look combined with his broad shoulders. Too bad he doesn't know I exist, we would make a fabulous couple."

Even though Era was a deity of a sort, she is restricted to the realm of Medio unless she is invited by the other governing Gods into their domains. The opposite is true as well, given that Era is the sole God-like figure of Medio, it is possible that her permission would grant them access to the realm. Meanwhile, she can not leave this dimension.

As the conversation progresses, Opal eventually dozes off into a deep sleep. Era watches her intently. She approaches her and pokes at her skin, touches her hair, explores her ears and toes, until she accidentally tickles Opal's foot and gets kicked straight across her face. That kick knocked an idea into Era's head. For the moment, she allowed Opal to rest while she devised a plan.

Era drapes over her daybed and turns the television to her favorite show, the first duel between Deus and Dannato. She marvels at Dannato's sweaty and messy hair while he swings his sword impeccably against Deus's bulky frame. Deus wasn't un-handsome, but his arrogance rubbed her the wrong way. Besides, she found him annoyingly plain. She was awed at the battle in the

Colosseum between the two Gods. She knew the ending by heart, and it still excited her every time she re-watched it.

CHAPTER 13

"How long did I sleep?" She rubs her eyes with her fists, her blurry vision inching towards focus.

The room looks just as before, with Pearl's shards still decorating the black and white checkered tile. She did not doubt that she likely had pillow marks on her face and dried-up drool on the side of her mouth. Well, maybe not, considering she was dead and all.

"I can fix her, if you'd like?" Era's smile grows wide with the suggestion. She stands by the entrance, with the sunset behind her accentuating her silhouette. She's tall, slim, and the epitome of elegance. She has trouble written all over her, and Opal senses it from miles away.

"What's the catch?" She is a skeptic of Era's good nature.

"Good girl, at least you know that nothing comes without a price. I'll make you a striking deal." She struts back with a slight bounce to her step.

"I'll repair your friend and give you a new outfit. That odious sack of potatoes just won't do it. It should burn in the eternal flame! In return," she sits next to Opal on the small daybed, twirling a strand of her hair on her index finger, "you give Dannato a letter on my behalf, the next time you see him." She winks with feline curiosity. Sitting gracefully with her legs crossed, leaning towards Opal, and with a snap of her fingers, grapes appear in her hand.

"If we are negotiating, I want you to help me remember how I died. Add that to your offer, and you have a deal."

"Negotiations? For free? HA! You don't have anything else I want, dear. My offer is already generous enough." Era's hand slaps the air, dismissing her request.

"Please, there has to be something I can do. I need to understand how it happened. Maybe I can learn from it and be of better help to others. Besides, you don't lose anything by doing this."

"I really shouldn't." Era folds her arms across her chest, actively avoiding Opal's puppy eyes. "Fine! Only because I find your cause mildly amusing and I sympathize ever so slightly. I'll give you one chance to prove yourself. One test of my choosing, if you pass, I'll show you, and if you fail, the previous arrangement stands. Deal?" Her eyes look down her nose, waiting for Opal to cower.

"We have a deal!" Opal sits up next to Era. "I can't believe you'll do all of this just to meet a man." She says with a giggle.

"Hey! He's not just any man. He's a God. And I'm so bored I'm tempted to keep you here forever, but I much prefer him."

Era snaps the bushel of grapes she was holding into a glass of wine. She ponders with each sip what kind of test she will give Opal. It is a difficult task to examine a person's judgment and character. She is aware of what kind of person she is through her actions in the afterlife. Justice ran her heart, but would she be able to take responsibility for her own wrongdoings on Earth? Would she be able to call out her own bullshit, or will she witness herself be dishonorable and turn a blind eye?

"I got it!" Era says with excitement.

"You got what?" Opal asks.

Without a word, Era responds to Opal's question with a snap of her fingers. She collapses backwards onto the daybed and trails a lucid dream.

"We'll see if you are as perfect as you think." Era relocates to her own daybed, sits back, and sips her wine. Through her television, she watches everything unfold.

CHAPTER 14

It is a sunny day in Tucson, Arizona. The dry heat felt as she remembered. Opal stands outside apartment 101, a familiar place she shared with her cousin. She doesn't know what year or time it currently is, but she strolls inside anyway.

It's a small white apartment with worn-down appliances, grey laminate flooring, major cracks in the paint, and the lingering smell of cigarette stench creeping in through the vents from her neighbor's apartment. Her dog, a copper husky, lies sleeping in the corner of the futon couch, and her cousin's chihuahua doesn't bark. They both did not sense her, which could only mean one thing: she isn't really there. Strutting towards her room, it looks just as she remembered too: grey comforter, no bedframe, and haphazardly installed white curtains.

A few hours go by, and Opal waits around for a while until she takes a look at the time. It's seven in the afternoon, meaning she was likely supposed to be at work. She followed her usual route to work, although walking, as she did not have a vehicle. Luckily, it was only about a twenty-minute commute on foot.

She arrives at the hospital where she works, and she gets an odd feeling, like she's being pulled. She followed that feeling all the way up to the seventh floor, where she found herself. She was sitting with a patient who required one-to-one observation.

"Oh God! That's me!" She rams through the door, and it doesn't open. She simply walks through it. It's dark in the room, and that version of herself is sitting on a chair with her bright phone in her hand, softly illuminating her face. The patient is sleeping peacefully in his bed, occasionally turning and changing positions. He was stable, and she found it appropriate to share attention between the patient and the small device in her hands. Messages were flowing between her and a boy. Her phantom self takes a peek.

"Robin, I remember him. He was the sweetest– " Memories flood her mind, foreshadowing what she was about to witness.

"Era, you wouldn't?" She rolls her eyes.

She watched their messages, back and forth. Opal knew she wasn't ready for a relationship, but she liked his attention and the way he treated her. She continued entertaining the idea, thinking it was harmless, truly trying her best to feel some sort of attraction to Robin, but she couldn't force herself to like him. Instead, she did what any narcissist would do.

Over the course of some time, Opal saw in third person how things progressed. Robin had fallen in love with her and had gone to great lengths to show her how he felt. Her heart pleaded to her to stop leading him on. Guilt lingered in the back like an afterthought. She had one excuse to keep Robin stringed along, Loneliness.

"You're so fucking selfish." She says as a matter of fact to that version of herself.

The facade continued for a while until Guilt kicked her in the head hard enough, making her feel disgusted with herself. She had decided to stop leading Robin on, but the damage was done. The boy was heartbroken; she used all the textbook narcissistic excuses to make herself feel better. Scapegoating her Guilt by blaming him and his gullibility.

The memory finally stops, like a movie that was paused mid-show. A small menu appears suspended in mid-air with only two options.

"Change or Erase"

This was the test. Changing something would require her to acknowledge that she wronged someone. Erasing it would be easy, selfish, and avoid the existence of the issue in general. It would be simpler to forget this happened, to pretend she was perfect and always only the victim. In the afterlife, Opal was a victim of her own wrongdoings and more or less Rogue influence. But had she ever considered her own villainess in others' stories and her own? She had come to the realization that sometimes we are our own Rogue. Guilt didn't plague her until she committed an action that elicited that feeling in the first place. And, although that wasn't the case for all situations, the first step to rehabilitate herself was to acknowledge there was a problem in the first place.

Her finger gently presses on the button labeled "Change," effectively taking her back to the moment this whole situation began, in the room of the patient with her phone in her hand. She saw herself sitting in that same chair, messaging Robin. She gently approaches herself and taps her shoulder, freezing her in the chair. She takes the phone from her hand and writes out a message:

> "Hey Robin, first of all, thank you for taking the time to get to know me. I appreciate all your efforts. Unfortunately, I am not ready for a relationship, and I am simply not interested in you like that. I am sorry for leading you on and lying about my intentions."

Opal presses send and waits for the response that never came.

CHAPTER 15

"I was such an ass for doing that to him." Opal rambles to Era.

She had woken up feeling like the scum of the realm, disgusted by her own actions. She had pondered this exact moment of her life while on Earth, literally trying to forget about it.

"I was surprised you chose to change your story. I would have done the same, but more so for the plot." Era's glass reverts to a bushel of grapes. "I agree, though, it was a major dick move to lead that poor human boy on. He was so cute and sweet to you. He really did not deserve it."

"I know, I know. Why do you think I feel so bad about it? I knew I was wrong the whole time, I was just too selfish to do anything about it."

"Yeah, and you have the audacity to think you don't deserve your sentence. Maybe you should listen to your little friend Judas." Era wiggles her brows.

"All I'm saying is that nullifying a judgment isn't fair, not to me, not to Judas, not to anyone. How does one action dictate our entire existence? Also, how do you know Judas?" The sound of his name still elicits a flutter in her chest. Opal grabs the back of her hand where he had given her a sweet parting gift, and with it she touches her cheek.

"Okay, okay, relax. I get what you're fighting for. I wouldn't be helping or bargaining with you if I didn't. As for Judas, all you need to know is that I'm rooting for you two." She winks.

Opal's cheeks go bright red, considering she had no blood flow; it was a true testament to the butterflies in her non-existent stomach. She did think of him, occasional flashbacks of her first days, and the way he's helped her so far. She could be imagining things, but she was almost sure that she elicited the same feelings in him as well. Too bad they were dead, there is no way of knowing if they'll get to see each other again. She thought of how much she wanted to hold his hand again. With a shake of her head, she decides to change the subject.

"So, did I pass?" Opal asks with a huff and puff.

Era, clearly amused by her fluster and loss of composure, responds.

"You passed. You have proven to be capable of acknowledging and learning from your actions. Without those two qualities, it would be pointless to show you your memories. Also, it was mirthful to witness how messy you once were." She snorts, followed by a plop of a single grape.

"Now, as promised–" Era leans back.

"Are you going to make me fall asleep again? The whole no warning thing is starting to get exhaus–" Mid sentence, Era snaps her fingers, once again landing Opal in a profound sleep.

She has never meddled in any case like this. In a sense, Era understood why Judas helped her in the first place; there was something endearing about her. Her gaze softens as she watches Opal sleep. It is safe to assume that the Gods are searching for her, likely with a posse of Reapers on her tail. Era thought, maybe in another reality where they were both humans, they could have been friends. A small beam of light reflected from the broken blade on the ground, breaking her pensive state.

"Well, I might as well get to work." For once, Era was not interested in watching someone's story. It didn't feel right to indulge in this kind of suffering. Opal had left an impression through her actions and the way she nonchalantly spoke her feelings. Era thought her admirable, but she would never tell her that.

CHAPTER 16

Three Weeks Before Death

Opal wakes up tucked into her messy bed at the apartment complex College Heights, Tucson, Arizona. She had worked the night before, as evidenced by the crust in her tear ducts. The pandemic still ran rampant in the world, and her shifts had become grueling. In the midst of all the chaos, there was one thing she looked forward to: a boy. Tall, blonde, and handsome, he worked at an after-school program at a nearby elementary school. Their relationship had started through a mutual friend a few months ago. They quickly became familiar with each other, going on dates, outings, and having sleepovers.

She quickly got ready and ran out the door. In the parking lot, Sebastian sat at the wheel of his 2012 silver car. Trotting down the stairs in a flowy button-up shirt, short jean shorts, and a slick back bun, Opal was excited for their date. Together they rode up a few hours towards Mount Lemon, a beautiful mountain formation famous for the fall foliage. That day, they explored the cabins, the gift shops, and ate some snacks together at the famous cookie shop. They spoke about many things, including a recurrent topic.

"We don't have anything in common," Sebastian says as he takes a bite from his chocolate-chip cookie.

"We like each other, that's all we need to have in common." Opal bites her white-chocolate macadamia nut cookie.

They have had multiple conversations about this topic. Sebastian had been expressing feelings of not being enough, and she was trying her best to reassure him. Opal was in love with him and was desperately trying to make things work. Despite having to constantly reassure him, she was hopeful of a serious relationship developing.

On the drive back, Opal began feeling tired and slightly light-headed, attributing it to the high elevation. The alarming concern was brushed off. That night, while they were both in bed, another conversation about his feelings sprang forth again, resulting in a break from the unofficial relationship. Through the hardships of being apart, they attempted to complete the daunting task of being apart from one another. A few days passed, and they were still in constant communication, breaking their own rules, leading to the eventual cave to temptation multiple times, without setting clear boundaries. They rekindled their situationship and went on more dates, both unclear of their intentions or the status of their relationship. However, Opal knew very well how she felt about him. Love was an undeniable feeling that she couldn't keep contained.

◆○◆

As time passed, they scheduled dates, including the one for today. Opal changes clothes whilst getting ready for their dinner date. She notices her breasts becoming tender and enlarged. She takes a moment to think about the feeling, realizing she doesn't remember when her last menstruation was. Considering she has been irregular all her life, she didn't think much of it, but a small thought lingered in the back of her mind. She hops into her blue 2016 car and drives to Sebastian's place, where he is cooking dinner for her. They had good yet dry chicken breasts and some unexpectedly delicious asparagus, accompanied by mashed potatoes. They ate, they conversed, and finally cleaned up.

He was washing the dishes while she cleared the table. Opal stopped every few minutes to rub at her aching breasts. He notices on their way to the bedroom.

"Goodness, my breasts are so tender." She says.

Sebastian is following close behind, and a movie night after dinner is waiting for them.

"Yeah, I noticed you rubbing at them. Why are they tender? Are you getting your period?"

"I don't think so," she runs her hands over them gently, "but I could swear they also look bigger. Do they look bigger to you?" She asks.

"Honestly, yeah, a little." He surveys them.

She laughs somewhat hysterically. "What if I'm pregnant?"

Their eyes meet, exchanging a moment of pure terror.

"Oh…my…God…What if I'm pregnant?" The realization sinks in, sparking shocks of Anxiety running through her chest and limbs.

The next few moments consisted of a long conversation rationalizing the possibilities and vast amounts of online searches about the signs and symptoms of pregnancy. They came to the conclusion that they would not be able to sleep in peace until they knew for sure, so they decided to go to a twenty-four-hour pharmacy and buy a pregnancy test. The drive there and back held a deafening silence and a tension that could be cut with a knife.

She bolts to the bathroom immediately following the instructions of the pregnancy test. She sets it down on the counter while she cleans up. She turns it around; a strong line and a very faint one appear side by side. She shows Sebastian.

"The box says that two lines mean positive even if it's faint." She says.

Sebastian bites his nails, slightly rocking on the edge of the bed.

"I think you should take the second one. I read online that false positives are a thing." He replies.

She waits for a minute, maybe even hours, gulping down as much water as she can handle. For the second time, she enters the bathroom, completes the test, and waits until the exact time instructed on the box passes. She turns the test around, and two solid black lines stare at Opal and Sebastian.

"It's positive." She breathes out.

He plops himself on the edge of the bed, rubbing his face incessantly.

"I just learned how to have sex." Are the first words that escape his mouth and the ones she will remember forever. Those were the first words that came from the man she loved when facing this challenge. A phrase that to her indicated he was only thinking of himself and how this situation affected only him.

"What should we do?" He asks.

"I don't know." She caresses her lower belly.

"I'm not ready to be a dad. I mean, look where I live." He points to his crummy bedroom with its crusty carpet and dull blue comforter.

They have a conversation, and together they decide to wait until tomorrow to make a decision. They were in denial, so they wanted to play into the small possibility that this was a false positive.

"Let's go to Urgent care tomorrow. We can get a pregnancy test there and make sure this is one-hundred percent happening." She says.

Sebastian climbs into bed, not sure of how to process the whole situation, and eventually dozes off, filling the room with subtle snores. Opal couldn't rest, freaking out couldn't wait for her. The bed was too soft, she was sinking, drowning into it. The floor was too hard, but the soft rug was just right. The ceiling spun above her, dizzying her with the consequences of her own decisions.

◆━◯━◆

"Opal, right this way, hun." The lovely nurse escorts her inside. Sebastian stays behind in the lobby.

The results of the third pregnancy test were pending. Opal sat on the small plastic chair in the consultation room. She hoped the world would swallow her whole, thinking maybe if the building collapsed, it would take her with it. A moment later, followed by three knocks, a tall older man with a tapered beard walks in. He sports a long white coat and holds a paper in his hand.

"Congratulations! You're pregnant."He said with the brightest smile she had ever seen. In most cases, pearly white smiles would have been kind; to her, it felt sinister.

He proceeds to ramble on about prenatal vitamins, resources, and what to expect during the first trimester. Every word he says after that initial phrase enters one ear and exits out the other. Her world was falling apart, and her arms did not have enough strength to hold the sharp shards together. Pale and shaken, she walks to the lobby. Sebastian looked comically big compared to the waiting room chairs. The room was a light yellow, however in her memory, it was black and white and covered in cobwebs. Their eyes meet, her semblance confirms their fears.

The next few days happened too quickly for her to process. Together, they made the decision to abort the pregnancy. Even if it was a mutual decision, it still weighed heavily on her chest. Sebastian had become distant. They barely spoke to each other. All of a sudden, this whole situation was a waiting game until the day of their appointment at the clinic. They agreed to go together.

She kept herself busy picking up shifts at the hospital, working long hours through a global pandemic kept Opal distracted and Guilt tethered, for now. Every now and then, she caught a glimpse of herself in a mirror, and every time she would stop to admire her barely-there bump. She wondered each time if they were making the correct decision.

Alas, the day of the appointment arrived.

"Hey, I can't go to the appointment with you today. I'll still send you half the money, though." He said on the phone one hour before the appointment.

She was already there waiting in her car. Opal noticed protesters starting to rally. They held poster boards with graphic images and equally disturbing slogans. That was her queue to get inside before there were more of them. Scurrying through the small crowd, trying not to get caught in the middle, she makes it inside.

"This is the first appointment, nothing is going to happen, right?" She thought. Opal was under the impression that this would only include an ultrasound, a discussion about options, and maybe some action if she decided. Walking through the door, she notices the front desk, where she approaches and promptly fills out the forms. She sat in the waiting room for about ten minutes and was swiftly guided towards the consultation room.

The room had an examination table placed in the center of the room with stirrups at the foot. There was a beam spotlighting it; everything else was blurry. She was instructed to strip and gown up, but with every piece of clothing she removed, she felt like she shrank a size. Approaching the examination table felt like she was approaching a mountain that required a strenuous hike to mount. She did as she was instructed. Her back smashed the crinkly protective paper. Like the frogs in a chemistry class, she felt the white of the fluorescent lights expose her, and heard the soothing voice of the sonographer, who was applying lubrication to the probe, which sounded more like a butcher sharpening a knife.

The sonographer was gentle and empathetic. But no amount of warmth could make this moment less chilling. She inserted the probe, and with that action, her eyes welled. "How could you cry? How can you pretend to be the victim?" She thought. As the probe impaled her, searching for the embryo, her mind ran a thousand miles per hour, until the sonographer spoke again.

"I'm having a hard time finding it. According to your chart and the information you provided, you should be about six weeks along. It should be fairly easy to find…Oh! There it is! Small little bean, but–" She suddenly stopped talking. As a healthcare provider herself, she understood that in most cases, long silences do not bear good news. Opal had opted for no sound during the ultrasound, scared that she wouldn't be able to handle the guilt. The Sonographer clicks a few buttons and takes a few pictures of the ultrasound. Something was wrong. She felt the restraint in the worker, who gently removed the probe and helped her get cleaned up.

"The doctor will come and talk to you in a moment, hun." She says with a small downturn to her mouth and exits the room.

The provider struts into the room, taking a seat across from Opal. She wears a pair of black scrubs, a long white coat, and her hair is sported into a neatly tied French braid. She crosses her legs, followed by a modest sigh.

"I'm Dr.Genevieve," she shakes Opal's hand, "how do you feel?" She has empathy written all over her face.

She simply nods in answer to Dr.Genevieve's question, so the provider takes the hint and continues on.

"I'll cut straight to the situation. The embryo does not have a heartbeat." Her voice clipped and opened for questions.

"What does that mean exactly?" Opal responds, barely able to contain the crack in her voice. Her legs bounce and swing, motored by anxious thoughts.

"It means that as of now, the embryo is not growing. At this time during a pregnancy, there is usually a pulse and the amniotic sack is a proportionate size to the embryo, both of which indicate the possibility that it's not growing. Considering the size of the sack, it's likely the embryo stopped developing a while ago, which means that you have been pregnant for longer than we thought. You have a few options: you could wait and see if it develops, although the chances of possible severe fetal abnormalities and sepsis would increase, or you could terminate. I will give you a moment to think."

Dr.Genevieve stood and gifted her a moment of privacy to sift through her options.

"There isn't much to think about." Opal thought. The news was both a curse and a blessing; the decision was practically taken from her hands. But, the *what ifs?* Ringed at an alarming volume in her mind. Guilt beat her chest into a conclave. Anxiety made her arms tingle. Loneliness pushed her shoulders down. This was too much to process, but who could she call that wouldn't judge her? What could she do to make this better?

"You can't make it better."

"You'll be a murderer now."

"Look at you all alone, you thought he loved you? Where is he now?"

"It's your fault. Your fault. Your fault!"

Endless words rang in her ears, phrases that she thought of herself and likely what others would think of her if they knew. With a cold head, she decided to terminate now. Dr.Genevieve returned and patiently walked her through the process.

The process required three steps: a shot in the arm because she was an Rh-negative blood type, one pill to stop any further growth of the sack and embryo, and lastly buccal pills that would be taken at home the next day for expulsion.

After a sharp sting of a needle and the descent of a large pill down her esophagus, the first two steps were completed. She sat in the waiting room while the clerk finalized her paperwork and her bill. Opal calls Sebastian with no response. She messages him instead and informs him of the plan for the following day. He responded promptly and said he would be there. Her card swipes on the reader, paying for the services and pharmaceuticals which she holds on to tightly while making her way to her car. Opening the front door of the clinic, she was confronted by about a dozen protesters holding signs and calling aggressive chants. The graphic images, the rage on their faces, and Opal's heart ready to fall out of her butt intimidate her. She readies herself and walks.

"MURDERER! MURDERER! MURDERER!"

They sing their words and preach their anthems, preying on her like vultures with a God-complex.

"Don't kill your baby! You'll go to hell!"

"She deserves to go to hell! God doesn't love baby killers!"

One lady approaches her on what seems like the longest walk to her car ever, yelling and yelling about the matter, until Opal couldn't bite her tongue any longer.

"It's already dead!" The crowd goes silent.

"Do you think I want to carry a dead child? Do you think I want this? Do you think I am enjoying this?!" The dams in her eye ducts finally blow, allowing a raging waterfall to decorate her face.

"You should have closed your legs, whore!"

"Shut up! Shut up! Shut up! You don't know anything. God does not favor ignorance, and I don't owe you any explanations."

There were no further answers from the protesters, even if there was, she wouldn't have been able to hear it with the intense ringing in her ears, making her deaf for the rest of the day.

The Next Day

Sebastian arrives at Opal's apartment. The place smells of instant ramen and burnt meat. She cooked up a mediocre meal and prepared as much as she could. Without knowledge of what to expect, she overprepared in supplies: heat packs, emesis bins, pain medications, and an inhuman amount of large menstrual pads. They played a movie following the placement of the pills as instructed by Dr.Genevieve the previous day. The final step began.

Long hours of intense cramping, nausea, and heavy bleeding passed. Shivers and cold sweats covered her body. Clouds fogged her mind, and incessant whispers plagued her ears.

"Murderer..."

"Pathetic..."

"Sinner..."

Desperate, she was desperate for comfort. She looked over to her left where he lies. Sebastian planted himself on the bed, looking through his bright phone, seemingly in conversation with someone. He was there, but he wasn't. His physical body was present; his mind was not. Opal noticed this, preoccupied by the intense cramping, she cared less and less as the hours passed.

After the third movie ended, she decided to take a shower, assuming it would help soothe her pain. Hot scorching water rained on her while she sat on the cold shower floor. She pleaded to God to let this scalding water burn away her sins. She prayed for God to forgive her. She prayed to God to send her child to a family that really wanted it; she thought it deserved a good life. And, although the decision was not entirely hers, her Catholic guilt continued rubbing her soul raw. Opal hugs her knees and rocks back and forth, back and forth.

"I'm sorry. Please forgive me. I know I am not worthy of asking, but please...please." She sobbed.

Her fingers and toes pruned like raisins, she stood barely able to contain her own weight when she was plummeted by a con-traction, forcing her to brace the tile wall to prevent hitting the ground. All of that, followed by a resonating plop sound.

"Oh God. Oh God." She pleaded. "I'm sorry."

Opal peeks to confirm what she thought. On the ground of the shower, a palm-sized red blood clot with a tiny speck, the size of half her pinky nail, stared right at her. It was done. This was over. There is no turning back from the precipice she was falling from; Guilt cracked the floor of her soul, and she slipped right through it. Her soul grasped and clawed at the walls of her body, trying to stay afloat. Her glassy eyes clear, and after a moment of recollection, she steps out of the shower, dries off, and gets dressed in an oversized shirt. Her dripping hair leaves a trail while she makes her way back to the bed to fall apart in the comfort of Sebastian's arms. But, when her head landed on the pillow, and his arms encased her broken shell, her life continued to fall apart.

It could have been the way she was so still from the bottomless numbness that consumed her body that he thought she was asleep. He opened his phone in front of her face and showed her a truth she didn't have the energy to acknowledge. There was nothing left for her to feel.

"Murderer. Murderer. Murderer." Keeps ringing in her ears.

The following day, she regained some strength and once and for all ended things with Sebastian. The succeeding weeks brought complications and a hospital visit. Fragments of the amniotic sack were left inside her, causing her to continue bleeding, putting her at risk for sepsis and hemorrhage. She was utterly alone because she couldn't bear to tell another soul about her sins and failures yet. It was too soon, so she opted to message Sebastian. A small conversation sprouted regarding her hospital stay.

"I'm scared." She messages him, followed by an automated response from the application they used to communicate.

"The following message cannot be viewed by the recipient."

She was left to sulk in her own disaster, alone—

CHAPTER 17

Two Weeks Before Death

Throughout the course of the post-abortion complications, Opal was also having academic and financial turmoil. Schools had turned to online learning in the midst of the pandemic, affecting millions of people around the globe. She had volunteered to work the affected units in the hospital and picked up extra shifts as a result of the financial hardships. After some time working this schedule and navigating her personal life catastrophes, she had forgotten she was taking classes at all. Until today, while she sat in a hospital bed waiting for her discharge paperwork to go home after her post-abortion complications, she received an email stating:

To Whom It May Concern,

The current student registered under the name Opal Tempest is under academic probation for unsatisfactory grades at the time of completion of the enrolled courses for the Fall 2020 semester. Contact your academic and financial advisors regarding how to move forward.

– Best Regards from

The University of Amarillo

This whole time, she was so worried about her personal life: a failed relationship, an abortion, a broken heart, losing precious family members to the pandemic, working in the most depressing and stressful environment she has ever endured, and now this. She has hit rock bottom, and she has never felt worse than in this moment, both physically and emotionally. Opal's shoulders strained with the pull of tight knots and chronic pains, whilst coming to the realization that there wasn't much to do in this situation.

She was studying to become a Doctor, but through her years in healthcare, she had realized that was not the right career choice for her. She was lost and neck deep in student loans to give up everything she had worked so hard for. Although she felt everything had given up on her already. She sits in the hospital studying the room, admiring the sunlight filtering through the window, and to her surprise, the sunrays are not warm, they feel cold instead, as if the world was telling her even warmth was unattainable for her, like she was not worth spending that energy on. Opal felt the world reject her, and the voices in her ears confirmed those thoughts.

"Another failure? Not surprising."

"Disappointment."

"Maybe you should put an end to the pain once and for all."

"The world would be so much better without you anyway."

"Failure."

With a small wave of determination, she tried to better her situation, although her efforts were fruitless. The weight of embarrassment threatened to fully submerge her under a dark, murky water like a heavy anchor tied to her feet. She allows herself to collapse and crash onto the flat pillow and cardboard bed, pressing forward, ignoring that hopeless feeling growing in her chest. Using her phone to endlessly search the web for possibilities: How to go bankrupt? How to figure out what I want? How to pick myself up after hitting rock bottom?

Her incessant efforts resulted in no answers, more questions, and more anxiety. Her parents would be a great resource, but she was not ready to talk to them about this. Tragedy had struck their family with the death of three family members at the hands of the rampant virus. She thought they didn't need another burden. There was no choice but to keep working long hours at the hospital and try to accumulate as much money as possible. Opal thought she could use work as a distraction from her enormous failures. Her employment turned out to be a momentary life jacket barely keeping her head afloat.

Opal takes a deep breath and uses her phone to drop out of the University, followed by a feeling of impending doom. She felt the shift in her energy when she made that decision. She felt her limbs go numb and her eyesight blur. Within the newfound discomfit, there was an odd comfort from it, letting her mind and body run on autopilot seemed to fix her current problems.

She was discharged from the hospital and headed to her local pharmacy to pick up her prescribed medications and a box of her favorite antihistamines. Her favorite brand was Benarul, which always helped her sleep after a tireless night at work. Her feet move on their own, followed by her hands, and the voices in her head continue to chant in her mind, creating the background tune for the rest of her days.

"Failure."

"End it."

"Failure. Failure. Failure."

"End it. End it. End it."

CHAPTER 18

One Day Before Death

Opal wakes up at around four in the afternoon, readies herself for work in her usual Ciel blue scrubs and slick back bun. She usually receives a message about the assigned unit she will be working on that night. Being a nursing assistant in the staffing services and in the float pool meant that she went where she was needed. During a worldwide pandemic, that meant the virus-infested units. It was those units that needed all of the extra personnel, at first she had volunteered to work those units, but with time, it resulted in less of a choice and more of a need.

The intensive care unit of the South location of Badger Hospital was waiting for her. This unit was compact, with only twelve beds and a high turnover. It was surrounded by a rural and underserved population; it was unsurprising that the death rate in this location was high.

She strolls in sporting waterproof shoes, and her recycled N95 mask on hand in her paper bag provided by the hospital. There was a shortage in personal protective equipment due to the high demand. Marks and irritation already ornament her face around the bridge of her nose, cheekbones, and behind her ears from the constant tugging of her masks. Her undereyes bore cavernous purple bags, a gift from the sleepless nights.

Lately, her body worked on autopilot. Her feet knew where to take her, her hands knew what tasks to do, muscle memory was in full control, driving the vehicle, while the bitter-sweet whispers still poisoned her ears.

"Don't you get tired of this?"

"You only get in the way; the hospital is better without you."

"Stop whining, no one wants to listen to that."

"Nuisance."

"Disappointment."

"End it. End it. End it."

The night began as it usually did. She starts by taking reports from the outgoing nursing assistant on all twelve patients. Followed by constructing her "To do" list for the night, and penciling in morgue duty. This was during the second wave of the pandemic, with a surge in mortality, the morgues in hospitals had become saturated all over the globe; this hospital was no exception. This specific hospital had a smaller morgue. It consists of one un-refrigerated room holding two large freezers that have the capacity to hold six bodies each at a time, obviously not enough room. The temporary solution was to assign staff, such as nursing assistants, to aid security in the rotation of bodies in and out of the freezer to prevent thawing.

Moreover, all twelve patients had the rampant virus, some form of pneumonia, or other respiratory complications thrown in the mix among their pre-existing conditions. All twelve were intubated and on mechanical ventilation, meaning that a machine was essentially breathing for them. The first half of the night played out as usual: vital signs, blood sugars, bed baths, repositioning, when the witching hour struck. It might have been the full moon or a cruel prank from the Gods above when all hell broke loose.

Room one begins to alarm. A deathly rhythm rings on the monitor, and in that half of a millisecond, about half the staff rushed to the room. What they all saw was desaturation, cyanosis, agonal breaths, and upon placing two fingers on the patient's neck, a pulseless heart. Chest compressions were launched, adding rib-cracking sounds to the symphony that is a code blue. The family of the patient was contacted via video call, and Opal held the electronic tablet serving as the bridge between their communication. The family instructed the team to stop interventions and let the patient pass peacefully. Visitations were not permitted to prevent the spread of the virus, so when the room cleared, Opal held the tablet for them to say goodbye. In her hands, she could feel their hearts reaching through the screen, their cries echoed as the slowing heart rhythm transformed into a flat line.

"Time of death 00:30 AM." The provider announced.

Without respite after exiting room one, room two was already being resuscitated. The family was not reachable. Chest compressions. Alarms. Doctors yelling orders. In the middle of this chaos, room three was actively declining, effectively splitting the team between the two rooms. Opal took turns as compressor for both rooms, running back and forth, trying to catch her breath between sessions. Eventually, the unavoidable happens.

"Time of death for rooms two and three 01:33 AM." The provider says.

Rooms four, five, and six had active "Do Not Resuscitate" orders established by their families or power of attorney, after they were already intubated. All three rooms began a waltz of lowering oxygen saturations. The dance quickly turned into a race competing for who could drop to zero the fastest. Oxygen 50%, 20%, and so on. Until all interventions were ineffective, resulting in three bodies being enveloped in a slight tinge of blue.

"Time of death for rooms four, five, and six is 02:00 AM." The provider projects.

The next six rooms followed the same progression. Each of them is doomed to a different version of the same fate. The staff is powerless against the will of their souls, and the illness is spreading through their bodies.

"Time of death 02: 42 AM."

"Time of death 03: 10 AM"

"Time of death 04: 22 AM"

"Time of death 04: 59 AM"

"Time of death 05: 00 AM"

"Time of death 05: 33 AM"

Every single nurse, nursing assistant, respiratory technician, and provider in the unit stood sweaty and out of breath. Opal sat on a random chair near the nurses' station, wondering how the world ended up in this situation in the first place. She looks at her hands, studies the lines on her palms, and realizes there is nothing there. She holds no power and no ability to help others or change the course of the situation in front of her.

"Useless."

"You're powerless."

"End it."

"What made you think you could help?"

For the first time in five years as a nursing assistant, no call bells beeped, no IV pumps rang, no monitors yelled. The unit was completely quiet. Every room is occupied by a corpse that is not yet bagged or prepared for the morgue; there was no room anyway. Every staff member littered the unit, some with their heads in their hands, some bent over a trash can about to wretch, some standing still in complete shock. The lights were dimmed as they usually were during that time of the night, fitting the obscurity of the events of that night.

The clock rang, and it was 06:30 AM. Morgue duty does not spare anyone. Opal stands and lets her feet drag her to where she needs to go. Her semblance matches the twelve corpses tucked in their beds, while a chill runs down her back as she walks past them. She arrives at the morgue and helps the guard rotate the cold bodies out of the freezer and the next bodies into it.

"Hey, uh...you come from the ICU, right?" He asks.

He was a tall man with a rounded figure. He was usually very cheerful when he made his rounds around the units. Any other night, he would have cracked a self-deprecatory joke about his balding head. Lately, his shine dulled, and his eyes mirrored Opal's glassy nature.

She can't even muster an answer, only a subtle nod in response.

"I'm sorry, I heard what happened there tonight. Get home and get some rest, okay." He walks past her and gently pats her shoulder in reassurance as he heads back to his guarding post.

Opal stands in the empty corridor of the basement next to the morgue. All of a sudden, that room felt a lot more comforting than any other room in the hospital; the only room where people rested peacefully. As she exited the building, she was greeted by a colorful sunrise mocking the mopery that clouded her life. She headed for the pharmacy and bought a box of Benarul to help her sleep.

CHAPTER 19

Opal arrives home and tosses the small grocery bag with a box of Benarul onto her messy desk. She throws herself onto the top of her mattress, falling asleep in uniform and her filthy shoes, no longer caring about the germs crawling onto her bed. Her head hit the pillow, and sleep gave way.

A horror movie played through her dreams, depicting her night in the hospital and the events of the last three weeks. She was a helpless girl with no one to turn to for help at point Nemo, and instead of jumping into an ocean of shame, she stayed on her sinking ship and waited for the tow to take her with it. In this dream, there was no sound or background music, only the echo of the guard's words playing like a bullhorn and a broken record. But as the dream progressed, his voice changed into multiple sinister voices, breaking his sentence and infiltrating with their own.

"Get home and get some rest, okay."

"Get home...*End It!*...and get some rest, okay."

"*Failure*...Get home and get some rest, okay."

"Get...*END IT*...home and get...*END IT*...some rest, okay."

"*END IT!*"

The broken phrase of the security guard rang through her dreams. Images of the last few weeks continue to flutter like a shuffling deck of cards. Finally, the poisonous words infiltrating the guards' words took over completely. The slimy, eerie voices with constantly changing timbres and tones, as if one hundred people were speaking to her all at once, saying different things and eliciting different physical responses from her.

"You're useless." Her chest begins to hurt.

"End it."

"What made you think you could make a difference?" Her head starts to pound.

"Do it. Make yourself sleep forever. Just a few more of those pills."

"You couldn't even keep life inside you alive. Pathetic." The haunting voice has the audacity to laugh, and her stomach twists with the gut-reaching sound.

"End it, Opal!"

"End it. You can rest with us."

"You felt it yourself. You felt how death is so peaceful."

"Do it, Opal! End it, Opal!"

Her heart raced at the rhythm of horse hooves hitting the ground of a race, but instead of a racecourse, it was her chest, startling her awake. She is covered in sweat, her bun barely hanging on top of her head. And, a headache so raw she had to press her temple for a few seconds before she could stand. Without a thought, she grabs her keys and heads to the pharmacy to buy some Benarul to help her sleep. Slowly walking through the pharmacy isles she finds the antihistamine section where she grabs a box and places it in her basket.

A light mist of rain covers the back of her neck, smelling like strong alcohol and disinfectant spray.

"Are you shameless?! You're putting everyone at risk wearing that here!" An angry lady clutches her facemask and sprays the disinfectant spray on her again. Opal openly stares at her with a fixed gaze.

"Hello…" the lady waves her hand in front of Opal's face, trying to elicit a reaction, "are you there? Ugh! I need a manager!" The woman walks away angry, demanding a manager.

Opal couldn't help but think that the lady had a point, but she couldn't muster the will to care. Absent-mindedly, her arms pull another box of Benarul and throws it into her basket. Paid. Bagged. Got behind her wheel, and in the blink of an eye, she now stood in her room. On her desk sit two boxes of Benarul. In the bag, she holds another two. She places all four of the boxes side by side.

"Get home and get some rest, okay." Stuck in her mind, similar to a piece of gum on her shoe, followed by the haunting whispers she was not yet accustomed to.

"Do it!"

"End it."

She dumps two pills from one of the boxes into her hand and lands them in her mouth.

"Get home and get some rest, okay."

"End it, Opal."

"Failure…Useless…"

She mouths the rest of the pills from that box and swallows.

"Get home and get some rest, okay."

"Keep going, you're almost there."

"More. More. MORE!"

Opal opens the second box and does the same.

"Get home and get some rest, okay."

"MORE!"

"END IT"

"DO IT!"

The third box is now empty.

"Get home and get some rest, okay."

"MORE. MORE. MORE!"

"FINISH IT."

"END IT!"

All contents of the fourth box lay in the palm of her hand. Her eyes roam the room one time, admiring the details of her bedroom. The pretty sunrays filtering through the curtain delicately highlight the pictures of her loved ones decorating the room. All while caressing her lower belly.

"Okay, I'll get some rest now." Are her final words.

The handful of small pink pills enters her mouth, and she chugs water to help them down. In a matter of minutes, her vision blurs as she stumbles towards the balcony past the living room. She sits on her most frequented patio chair and watches the painted sky adorned with bright yellows and oranges. She noticed how dark hues of blues and purples slowly embraced the sun as it set. Her eyelids grew heavy. Her breath shallows. And, with one final breath, a single crystalline drop escaped her eyes as her sight was eternally set on the sight in front of her, for the last time. For the first time in months, Opal was finally resting in peace.

CHAPTER 20

"It took you long enough." A familiar voice rings in Opal's ears.

It takes a moment to realize where she is and who is talking to her. She feels the soft velvet lining of the daybed and the cushion underneath perfectly molding to the front of her body. The dim sunrays from the sunset filter through the canopied fabrics, waking her from her lucid dreams.

"Wake up. We have a deal, remember..." Era says.

Opal feels a small, round object hit her head, followed by her eyes completely opening. The bright light throws her head in a circle. She finally saw it. She knows everything. Another soft, round object hits her head again.

"Strop throwing grapes at me!" She rubs her head.

Era giggles and throws another one.

"How long was I out?" Opal says, shielding her face from the grape bullets.

"About three Earth days, not long in our time." She shrugs in response, finally stopping the air raid of grapes. "Was it what you expected?" she asks.

"Honestly, I didn't think I would actually go through with it. I was always passively suicidal. I never thought of actually hurting myself for the sake of my loved ones, but every day I woke up secretly hoping something would put me out of my misery. Life got hard, and my body began reacting to my emotions on its own accord. I was stuck, and in that moment, suicide seemed like the only way out."

"Rogues are very persuasive, especially when you have that many following you and pestering you. You didn't have much of a fighting chance." She swirls a strand of white hair on her index finger. Era lies patiently on her side next to Opal, patiently waiting for her to rise. "Did you learn anything?" she presses on.

"I'm not quite sure. I'm still processing all of it. I'll let you know when you visit me in the Underworld with Dannato holding your hand." Opal winks, now leaning up on her elbows, whereas before she was prone on the daybed.

"That's fair. Humans are incompetent in processing emotions effectively and quickly. By the way, I have something for you." The white-haired deity says.

"Let me guess, you made me some fancy suit?" Opal raises her brow, doubting it would be to her liking.

"See for yourself." She points to a manikin's bodice.

At a glance, it looks like a silver leotard with a high neckline. Up close, you could see the intricate chainmail surrounding the bust areas and notice that the neckline was a slightly darker metal. It had dainty cap sleeves made of dark, forest green fabric with swirls embroidered on the edges. The abdomen is a steel corset with subtle ridges around the hips. A pair of matching knee-length, steel boots with the same swirls as the cap sleeves embossed on the lateral. Next to it was the most beautiful scythe she had ever seen, vibrating harder as Opal's fingers ran through the blade. She might have tickled it the wrong way as the base bends and the flat side of the blade softly hits the top of Opal's head.

"Pearl!" The blade vibrates in response.

"Oh my God! You fixed her, and she looks so pretty!" Opal picks the scythe up and begins to steadily get accustomed to the new weight of the scythe. What used to be a wooden handle is now a matching steel handle to her whole ensemble.

"Go on now, try on your new outfit." Era instructs as she points behind the television.

"Can't you just snap your fingers and have me changed?"

"Yes, I can, but where's the fun in that?" Era replies.

It only took a few minutes, considering it was mostly made of metal, it was surprisingly comfortable. Once it was on, it put her curvy figure on display, a little too much for her comfort.

"I guess it's better than the cloak."

"You guess?!" Era almost spits out her wine. "It's a whole lot better. Now we can at least tell you're a woman, and I can sincerely say you look pretty hot. It'll be way more entertaining watching you fight in this new outfit. Think of what your friend Judas might think when he sees you in this." She winks.

Even lacking blood could not prevent the flush on Opal's cheeks at that comment.

"Well. It seems like I have my work cut out for me. I will fight as long as I can get away with it. When I get caught, I'll make sure to give your future hubby your letter." She mounts Pearl onto her back, and a sense of relief washes over her now that her friend is fixed.

"You already know it! By the way, feel free to stop by if you need rest. Pearl knows the way."

"I don't know if I should be afraid or excited right now. Regardless, I hope I don't get caught before seeing you again." Opal says.

"Don't worry, I'll make sure to drag you out of hell for a day so you can attend our wedding." They both laugh at the joke.

Both are secretly hoping that it doesn't come to that. Era would never admit it, but having someone in her home has made her realize how lonely she actually is. She saw in Opal a friend, even if it were for a short moment.

Era hands her the letter, and she safely tucks it away into her corset. She swings the beak of her scythe and opens a rift with purples and pinks swirling at the edges of the familiar cat iris. One deep breath later, she steps through with her long, dark brown, and wavy hair flowing behind her when the rift closes.

"I'm rooting for you, friend." Era's words echo after her, although they never actually reach her.

CHAPTER 21

"This is preposterous!" Deus vibrates the chamber with his timbre.

"There is no need to yell. We can hear you perfectly clear." Dannato says for the tenth time during their debate.

The Gods have been discussing the situation of the "Rogue Reaper" for a few Earth days now, neither coming to a compromising conclusion. In the meantime, they dispatched small units of Reapers tasked with tracking down Opal. Judas, having the favor of the Gods, was placed at the head of the mission. Her whereabouts have become unknown, previously her scythe served as a tracking device to an extent, but it lost connection all of a sudden, making her capture a challenge.

All things considered, the Gods do not have the ability to enter Medio since they do not reign it. They must be invited by the ruling deity, and to their knowledge, there was no such being. This leaves them in a predicament where their only power inside the realm of Medio was mere search and seizure, and forming oversized rifts once in a while to specific locations. Medio is known to have endless pockets within the realm, some of which the Gods didn't know about. Medio has been meagerly explored and was used only for its intended purpose: guiding souls through Reapings to prevent them from getting lost. There was never a reason to explore it further until now.

"The girl will be found, and when she is, she will be held to a proper trial." Parity says barely above a whisper.

"She doesn't deserve a trial, nor is she worthy of judgment! First, she commits suicide, which our existing law states to be an inexcusable offense. Two, she has broken every imaginable rule since her arrival. Three, it is unfair to the other Reapers if she is the only one to receive judgment. Therefore, her sentence is appropriate, and dare I say not enough! Without consequence, we will be upsetting the balance of our perfect system." The golden angel's wing is tucked in tight against his back.

"Since when do you care about fairness, Deus? Besides, our system is far from perfect. I see this now. You might understand if you stopped snorting clouds so often, it's making you and your cherubs dumb. I'll break it down for you...again. Opal is the first to break the law, and with that, she has shed some light on a flaw that we oversaw. Your first and third points are reasonable, although I am beginning to think that committing suicide might not accurately depict a person's character, especially when they are coerced into it. She is the perfect example. This whole situation was triggered because of the love she has for her sister and the need to protect her. Her motives are good, and for that, I can not punish her. Her soul does not belong in the Underworld, and maybe some of the souls of the rest of the Reapers don't either. The law is outdated and unreasonable in the current situation." Dannato ends his rebuttal with a bite from his ruby red apple.

"Keep the cherubs out of this, Emo King! Rule breakers do not belong in Paradise. I will never allow her to rest in peace after all the chaos she has unleashed upon our realm! How could I reward a divine criminal? What about the other Reapers? It wouldn't be fair for them." Deus folds his arms across his broad chest.

"Ugh–Did you even listen to anything I said?" The God of the Underworld rubs his temple.

Parity sits watching as they argue, contemplating both of their sides. Her delicate white dress elegantly cascades over the borders of her white throne, creating an illusion of a waterfall.

"I agree with you on that, Deus. It isn't fair for the rest. The other Reapers were not given the opportunity to ever show the true nature of their intentions, or of their souls. They were forced into a system and silently complied out of fear of us. All of this leads me to one conclusion, that our law is flawed." Parity adds her words to the tug of war between Deus and Dannato.

"Our lovely Parity and I are on the same page, brute. Our law is flawed, and as Gods we are responsible for fixing it. Starting with that girl." Dannato throws a wicked smile at Deus, who only huffs and puffs in his seat. The Goddess of Purgatory launches a stern stare in the golden angel's direction, enough to get him to settle down.

"I still don't think anything needs to be changed. We only need to find a fitting punishment for her and move on." Deus glares through his brow bone, emerald green eyes piercing a hole through Parity's head.

"Keep looking at her like that, and we'll have bigger issues." Dannato breaks the tension by throwing the core of his bitten apple at his head, eliciting a delicate chuckle from Parity.

CHAPTER 22

Pearl holds sturdy after every strike. Opal has become accustomed to the new weight of her weapon; it only took a few encounters to get adjusted. Without the extra weight of her cloak, she is also faster and lighter. Together, they arrive at Reapings before the "soul-collecting baboons" as Era referred to them, giving themselves more time to fight off Rogues and avoid extra confrontations.

Third movement. Fourth Movement. Cycle of Life. Those three movements were constantly in rotation, occasionally she would try new combinations when she thought it appropriate to take the risk. She goes through grueling hours of scythe-wielding at a time, surprised that she doesn't feel as tired as she thought she would be. After every battle, encounter, and life saved, she thought of the red clock ticking, reminding her that her time was limited, and Opal wanted to make sure every second counted.

— ◆ —

A middle-aged man is absentmindedly driving down a winding road up the mountains. His hands loosely cover the wheel while his body drives on autopilot. His sight is out of focus with that usual glassy aspect to it. Anxiety's lightning-like body sends shocks up and down his thin limbs. Depression pokes at his abdomen with its upside-down crescent moon-shaped head. Guilt runs behind his vehicle, shaking the ground as it chases him around the rocky mountain. His PTSD was shaped like a shadow of a soldier wearing a military hard hat; it had dark orange eyes. Its body is devoid of features and pitch-black. It held a machine gun and shouted in his ear like a sergeant.

"YOU AREN'T ENOUGH SOLDIER!"

"USELESS SOLDIER"

"DISHONORABLE!"

All his Rogues pocked and prodded at him like a flock of birds fighting for breadcrumbs. Vultures are waiting for the man to die. PTSD sends a few rounds of shadow-bullets into the man's head, triggering trauma to resurface at the forefront of his mind.

The man thinks of his younger self in the Armed Forces. He is in combat in a country that stands in the center of political turmoil. His squadron has come face to face to the opposition, and violence was the only choice. Kill or be killed. With his weapon in hand, his squadron and he marched through the war zone. Ducking and running from bullets while keeping formation. After the enemy is defeated, they walk through only to realize this was a civilian area and in-nocent civilians were struck to death in the crossfire. Glassy eyes left wide open for eternity in the bloodied children and mothers littering the inside of the houses. Crimson red sprayed the walls and splattered the floors and debris around them. Shouts of those in agony and gurgling noises of those choking on their own blood.

"YOUR FAULT, SOLDIER!"

"Murderer. Murderer. Murderer." Guilt added after every stomp behind him.

"End it...End it...End it..." The rest added in unison.

Depression and Anxiety take turns punching his stomach, his chest, and sending shock waves of breathlessness through his lungs. The man was struggling to breathe. Every breath was shorter than the last. His breathing is shallow. His chest is heaving. His head is spinning. PTSD shoots a few more bullets into his head, triggering another memory, shouting like a bullhorn into his ears, and the rest of the Rogues whisper in comparison to no demise. They played a symphony of torture, pushing, and pushing, and pushing him to do what they wanted.

The man was transported to two years ago. He was driving a vehicle just like this one, a navy blue 2019 car, and he was driving under the influence with his squad mate. They had left the base to go to the downtown area of the city they were stationed at to blow off some steam and get rid of the nightmares. The night went by without issue. He got behind the wheel, thinking he wasn't too intoxicated to drive back to the base. After a few miles, he didn't notice how fast he was going and ended up toppling over. The vehicle turned over multiple times, spinning on its side until it hit home on the passengers side on a large tree. His sight went white, and he lost consciousness for a moment. He was brought back to consciousness by the sound of sirens nearing. He looked to his side to check on his comrade, but what he saw would haunt him to this day. His friend was impaled by the branches of the tree straight through the center of his chest. The car was upside down, leaving his face and neck to be covered in gore, and his eyes wide open, asking him, "Why me?" Lieutenant Regal was pronounced dead at the scene, and he was dishonorably discharged.

"DISHONOR, SOLDIER!"

"DIE, SOLDIER"

"WORTHLESS, SOLDIER!"

"End it...End it...End it..." The other Rogues sang along.

"Drive off the cliff, Stewart. Do it...Do it..." They kept chanting.

"DIE SOLDIER, DIE!"

"Murderer."

"It should have been you!"

"Do it...Do it...DO IT!" They chanted longer.

Opal arrives just in time before Stewart drives off the cliff. She interrupts their venom and the sergeant's yelling. Pearl's sloped edge draws an infinity sign in the empty space at their front, a move they had tried before, once creating a deadly figure eight. As moths are attracted to light, the infinity lures the Rogues to it and snaps Stewart from his trance, momentarily. He shakes his head a few times as the claws of his demons loosen. They pry their claws deeper, hitting the spots they know hurt most. PTSD continues to fire shots at his head, Opal intercepts the shadow bullets with the flat side of Pearl's blade. Depression, Anxiety, and Guilt ensnare their victim, readying for the birth of a new companion. Third movement, Pearl freezes all of them. One by one, she picks them off Stewart as one would with lice on someone's head. Ashy rain covers Opal's hair, and at the same time, Stewart gains control of his wheel and his life. He parks on the shoulder of the road and calls his wife sobbing, now with a second chance to reconsider and live.

❖

The next few battles were uneventful. They successfully defeated the Rogues without any signs of opposition showing up. It was eerie how much she was getting away with, and impossible to comprehend how three all-powerful Gods were unable to just reach their hand through a rift and pluck her right out. Every time she stops to think in between attempts, she ponders how different things would have been if she had never broken the rules in the first place. And, without failure, an angular face with prominent brows and cold hands enters her mind. The thought of their last interactions stirred her. she presses the back of her hand to her cheek, hoping remnants of his kiss were still there. She thought of his voice and the sadness he carries in his eyes. She winces every time his choking scar appears in her mind. Opal wonders what his life was like and how long exactly he has served as a Reaper.

Judas was a kind soul; she knew that, but she questioned how he was capable of running along his sentence without questioning anything. He carries so much guilt and remorse in the empty cavity that is his chest that there is no room for anything else. He helped her a few times already, and he told her he might not be able to keep helping her, that is, until he makes up his mind. The thought of him going Rogue made her sad and excited simultaneously. If he did, they could be Rogue together, she thought, and even if it was for a little while, she might get to know him better and spend time with him before burning in a never-ending boiling cauldron in Dannato's basement.

The following case is of a teen boy sitting in his father's garage, eyeing the weapon arsenal. Hopelessness, with its coreless, bird-like body flying and poking at his head. Loneliness with its long arms and legs whispering bitter nothings into his ears.

"End it...You won't be alone anymore."

Rage sits under the boy, a match lit with bright red flames, slowly consuming him completely inside. It burns bright and attempts to fully consume the boy with every singeing word.

"They did this to you. Get the gun. Get it. They deserve it!"

Revenge stands at shoulder height behind the boy, and an identical shadow of the boy rakes its large black claws on his back, yelling after each slash.

"Kill them first, Erik! KILL THEM!"

"Do it...Do it...Do it..."

Erik quickly goes to his father's room and opens the unlocked safe tucked in the closet. He opens the door. He looks at all the guns of different sizes and capabilities. The smallest revolver fits into his backpack perfectly, no one would know it was there. His hands work by themselves when he grabs a few rounds of ammunition. When his feet forced him towards the yellow bus, he could feel something in his chest trying to warn him that the voices in his head were lying. But his eyes were glossed, and he was now a vessel set for self-destruction.

"Kill them, Erik!"

"Then point the gun at yourself. You will not be lonely anymore."

"Do it! Make them pay!"

Opal arrives at the scene just as he mounts the school bus, making his way to the back of the bus. Erik lives a few blocks away from the school, making it the last stop. Pearl is immediately swung into action, pulverizing Hopelessness and Loneliness into a few slices, combusting into a rain of coal. Upon giving attention to Rage and Revenge, her friend vibrates in her hand.

"Shit–"

Third movement. Opal dances with Pearl, swinging it in the shape of a cross as quickly as she can, but not fast enough.

"Stop right there!" A few voices demand behind her.

"It's the law. By order of the Gods, you are to be apprehended." A group of Reapers hovers through a closing rift. They floated with their hoods covering their faces. "Cowards." Opal thought.

It was unbelievable how anyone could watch this carry on for centuries without ever being perturbed. How could someone turn a blind eye to such atrocities, especially when they are avoidable and not entirely autonomous in most cases? The third movement had bought her some time to interact. It won't be long until the effect wears off.

"Can't you see what is about to happen because of those monsters? They are the same monsters that plagued you and me, and they are about to be the cause of a mass murder if we don't do anything about it. Do you really want to be a bystander? Do you want to be just as guilty as they are for simply watching it happen? Doesn't this make you angry?!" Opal yells.

She can't see under their hoods. Their faces were covered. Their energy, however, changed, and they hesitated to move forward. Opal hoped and prayed that she got through to them.

"We can't–can't let you." One stutters.

"Cowards!" She responds, this time with her full chest.

There is no time left to keep persuading them. She decides to disregard their presence. She surges towards Rage and Revenge. Rage consumes Erik, turning him into a falling comet burning more intensely as it falls faster and faster towards destruction. Revenge claws fast and hard. If it could break skin, his back would be flayed with gore and covered in warm blood. They hold a tight grip on the boy, enough to keep his eyes glossy. The puppet him to their will and keep his hand on the revolver in his bag, waiting for the best moment to strike.

"Make them pay, Erik!"

"Put a bullet through their heads. Do it! Do it!"

"Put a bullet through your own, Erik. You won't get in trouble if you do that."

"End it!"

"Do it! Do it! Do it!"

"Kill them! Kill them! Kill them!"

"Kill yourself! Kill yourself!! Kill yourself!"

Opal needed to hurry. Erik's hand holds the weapon tightly in a bus full of his peers. He sits quietly observing his rowdy friends as they throw erasers and trash in his direction.

"Erik the Ferret! Erik the Ferret! Erik the Ferret!" They chant.

"Are you going to go pipi in your pants again?"

"Go cry to your mommy." They laugh, they chant, and taunt him.

Rage burns brighter, Revenge scratches deeper.

Two Reapers take the offense in Opal's direction at the same time. It's impossible to guess what would happen if she used her movements on them, she didn't want to hurt them afterall. She only wanted them out of the way and for them to see what happens after she interferes. Opal evades their attacks, and she throws attacks at the pestering Rogues instead. Third movement, she cuts a sign of a cross at her front and puts a pause on the demon's whispers and soothes their torture on Erik, she bought some time. Only then does she turn her attention to the Reapers attacking her. She uses the base of her weapon to fight them off. Through the steel base of Pearl's handle, as a cop would swing a baton, she hit her mark over and over. Swing to the right. Swing to the left. Hit their heads. Jam their stomachs. The steel clanked against their scythes when the Reapers on standby joined the fight.

"Stop this. I don't...want...to...hurt you!" She said between defense and attacks.

Their blades soar. Up and down, side to side. They dance a waltz of sharp blades and blunt handles. Two Reapers retreat as they ready themselves for a massive cord-cutting from the school shooting that is about to take place.

There is no time for pettiness, no time for a fight. This had to end now. The school is two left turns away, and the Rogues had regained their ability to move. She tries again. Third move—

CLASH!

Pearl is intercepted by the opposition. "Fool!" she thinks to herself, "they know the movement." Opal has no other choice but to try her new movement, except this time she named it.

"Infinity Eight!" she yells.

The glowing infinity sign gifts the boy temporary relief as Rage and Revenge are drawn to the light emitted from it. Their grip on Erik slackens, and the Reapers stand stunned as she performs a Hail Mary. She takes the opening. Rage and Revenge fight for control over Erik, burning hotter and clawing deeper.

"Do it now! Kill them! Kill yourself!"

"End it! End it! End it!"

"Now. Now. NOW!"

They have arrived at the school. His hand still holds the gun, and his finger hovers over the trigger. His eyes are still glossed, but his steps forward towards the exit of the bus are hesitant.

Opal attacked like a flickering strobe light, busting the cloudy venom from Erik's life.

"Cycle of life!" She yells.

Her hands hold Pearl's base study and are confident in the cyclone. The speed of the blade makes her spin and levitate. Only when she spins fast enough does she direct her attack at the parasitic Rogues. She spins, faster and faster. Opal is the eye of the storm, smashing into Rage and Revenge. She is a metaphorical bucket of ice water tossed over the boy, sending a shiver down his spine. His mind is free, his mind is clear, his mind is his own. He shakes in fear, although not of the bullies but of what he was about to do. His finger backs away from the trigger. His hand only holds the base of the revolver when he changes direction; previously, his target was the school courtyard, now he heads towards the yard duty teacher. He takes the gun out of his backpack and hands it over to the teacher.

What happens after doesn't matter at this particular moment, without waiting, Opal opens a rift and jumps. When she catches a glimpse of the red scar hovering through another rift onto the scene, fashionably late. She almost felt regret for leaving so soon, but she couldn't risk it if Judas had somehow changed his mind about helping her. She longed to hear his voice and feel his comforting hands on hers. But for now, the simple sight of him would have to do.

Back in the scene where the boy now sits in the principal's office, incessantly crying, waiting for his parents and the authorities. The Reapers watch how the story unfolds with the boy, unable to comprehend their own feelings about it. They are used to arriving at death's door, who knew interfering so little would make such a change in a story. Opal saved so many lives that day, and the Reapers noticed.

"It's different, isn't it?" Judas asks the floating Reapers, and only one of them responds while they watch Erik being hugged by both his parents.

"We forgot happy endings exist." The Reaper replies.

CHAPTER 23

After six weeks of Earth time, multiple confrontations and grueling battles, Pearl finally led her to Era's safe haven. Opal lands back at Era's palace to rest on her designated daybed and wakes up in the comfiest pajama set. They feel like silk to her touch, and they have small prints on them.

"Are those llamas on my pants?"

"Yes, I learned that they are popular in your world. I was trying to be kind to you. Be grateful." Era munches on a few grapes.

"I get that, but what made you think I would enjoy Dannato's face on them?"

"Why not? Cute, plus cute, equals cuter. Besides, I have matching ones!" Era stands to show Opal her matching set. Both have llamas and Dannato's face scattered all over, and they are made of the same silk material; the only difference is that Opal's is pink and Era's is black. They laugh together.

Opal takes advantage of the comfy pajamas and sleeps for a while longer. After she wakes up they have a conversion about how bad things are turning out. Opal has the idea to count out loud the positive things to try and make herself feel less depressed.

"You don't get sweaty bangs here." Era counts three on her fingers.

"I'm saving lives." Opal keeps adding after every point Era makes.

"You have a beautiful place to rest." Era counts four.

"You have a gorgeous and perfect afterlife bestie." She unfolds her fifth finger.

This cycle happened every few weeks when Opal went to "Eraland" to rest. She has provided her with the same daybed every time and allows her ample time to rest as often as she needs. Opal occasionally stays a little longer, trying to prolong the possibility of being caught, and Era relishes her company. Occasionally, Era interrupts Opal's brainstorming session with possible new scythe movements.

"The same four movements are getting boring and predictable. I really need you to start spicing things up. Next time try a heart shape and see what happens." She shrugs as Opal gets ready to leave again.

"Era, lives are at stake here! And I have far too many Reapers on my ass. Maybe I'll try a heart shape next time I visit Eraland."

"Oh come on! You know damn well I prefer that you call it Eratopia. Besides, it should be more exciting to try it out on the field. Pretty please?" She makes puppy eyes and bats her long lashes at the Rogue Reaper.

"I'll think about it." With a slim smile and a quick eye roll, Opal opens a rift.

"By the way, Ereland sounds way better." She sticks out her tongue and jumps through the portal.

A few cases later, an older man with Lewy body Dementia struggles. Opal recognizes him. He is a famous actor who starred in multiple childhood films. His voice is so familiar that she would recognize it anywhere. His face was missing the trademark smile he was known for. The disease affected his brain and caused emotional imbalances and behavioral symptoms. This man only had one Rogue, Delirium. This rogue was strong enough by itself as it was a side effect of the illness, and it could not go away unless the illness was cured. Delirium didn't need to manipulate him physically. It sat on his shoulder, playing into his thoughts.

It was small and fairy-like, made of charcoal black and pointy wings. It flew from one shoulder to another, whispering into his head and altering his reality.

"No one loves you, Henry."

"Your wife didn't say good morning today. She hates the sight of you."

"Your doctor didn't tell you to have a good day. He must hate you, too."

"Annoying...Pest...Burden..."

"The world won't notice if you die."

"Did you see the waiter roll his eyes at you? You really didn't? Because I certainly did, he probably hates you too."

"You see that belt?"

"Grab it...Grab it...Grab it..."

"Wrap it around your soft neck. It'll make you feel better. At peace."

"Do it! Do it! Do it!"

"Grab it now, Henry!"

Henry grabs the belt. Ties it around his neck. The pressure is slightly comforting in conjunction with his glassy eyes. The world seems softer with the pressure of the belt constricting his blood flow and oxygen.

"You see the hook on the ceiling?"

"Go to it…Go to it…Go to it…"

"Hang the other side of the belt there."

"Hang yourself! Hang Yourself!"

"Do it! Do it! Do it!"

"Now. Now. Now!"

"I promise, Henry. The world will love that you're dead."

Opal arrives as he walks towards a chair to reach the hook on the ceiling. The little minuscule Rogue on his shoulder is barely detectable. She follows its miry whispers and directs her hits in that direction. The tiny black creature moves so quickly and leisurely tries to avoid the attacks. Left shoulder. Right shoulder. One, then the other. Back and forth. Another swing and Opal hits home. The pest is cut in half, not pulverized. Like a symbiote, its body pulls itself back together. The Fourth Movement did not work on it.

Delirium mocked her with the way it regenerated after each attack. Not only did it resemble a flying roach, but it disgusted her equally if not more.

Third movement. Pearl slices through the space with the shape of the familiar cross. Somehow managing to freeze herself.

"How the hell did I paralyze myself?" She can move her eyes and her mouth. She watches as Henry climbs the chair and begins to tie a knot on the belt to hang it on the hook.

"Henry! Please don't do it!" She pleads.

He links the belt through the hook and hangs. Her arms and legs tense. The vein on her forehead bulges as she struggles with the paralysis, just like Henry is suffering through suffocation.

"I'm sorry, Opal."

"That voice." She thinks.

"I know your heart is in the right place, but I can't watch you hurt yourself with this case. My leverage with Gods has come to an end, and I am forced to bring you to them." That sulky and silky voice.

The voice that haunts her dreams and the voice she yearns for the most. His face emerges into her line of sight, his dark hair and purple under eyes on full display. He looks tired.

"Judas. Let me go now!" She shouts at him.

"I never meant for things to end like this. I truly wanted to help you. I tried my best to postpone this very moment. I sensed trouble from you the moment we met, and yet I admired the way you stand for what you believe. However, I think I deserve this sentence." Judas says.

"Just when I thought I might of got through to you. How could you do this? To me? To him? This is not his fault. It's a disease and Rogue persuasion." She emphasizes Henry with her brows. "Did you already make up your mind about my cause? Are you siding with the Gods?"

"You're right, this isn't his fault, but you won't be able to defeat that Rogue regardless." He says.

They both watch as Henry's body swings under the pressure of the belt encasing his neck. Judas rubs his scar at the sight. The string attached to his chest is tightly pulled, ready to be cut. He's struggling to breathe. His face is bright red and well on its way to being purple. His body twitches as he suffocates.

"Do you honestly think this is okay? That it's fair for those monsters to interfere but not us?" She yells while desperately trying to free herself from the third movement's hold. "You might think you deserve this sentence, but what about the rest. Judas, please!"

"I told you what I think is irrelevant. All of this is out of control. There needs to be some order. I don't know what to think. I was okay with it while I was numb, and then you came into the picture and—and I just don't know what's right anymore." He says, flustered between the two sides at war in his chest.

"Is what you think irrelevant, or are you too afraid of your own guilt? Reaping is a scapegoat for you, isn't it? Coward! You are not who I thought you were, Judas! You're a coward!" She continues to struggle. "Are you afraid of those three that call themselves Gods? Gods that let their creation suffer without protection or fair intervention, well, I'm not! I will gladly be punished knowing I did not stand by while others suffered, knowing that I am not their accomplice." Hauteur coats each of her words. The warm spot she felt for Judas was freezing over with a thin icy indifference. How could she even think that he was kind and empathetic? How could she think he was going to choose her side? How could she be so naive to believe that there was hope in a place like this?

Henry's legs loosen underneath him. He leans forward, his breaths are shallow as his eyes roll to the back of his head.

"Judas, please. Let me help him. I'll surrender afterwards. I promise." She begs.

She offers her eternity for his life, for a man that she has never met, but out of principle and love. Judas looks at her. He contemplates the moment. He sees her passion, that passion that moved him the first time he saw her in the judgment chamber. The way she speaks and acts from her heart. The selfless way she puts others before herself. "She's so brave." He thinks.

"I could let you go, but it would be of no use. You will not defeat this Rogue." He says, the beginnings of tears lining the water line of his eyes. "What she doesn't understand is that Delirium will not die until he does, and it isn't multiplied like the rest, it's simply born from a disease." He thinks to himself, and within that thought comes the realization.

"She's right! Henry's suicide is not autonomous but a by-product of his disease. He deserves judgment." Judas ponders. Too late, he needs to pick a side once and for all.

Opal carefully wiggles her fingers, starting to regain feeling in her limbs. With the effects of the third movement wearing off, she watched impatiently as Judas thought about all of this while poor Henry was losing the battle for his life.

"You're right, I am a coward. However, not for the reasons you think. Henry will die, but not because we didn't try." Judas changes course.

He flies straight for Delirium. A fly stuck in the spindles of a spiderweb under the weight of his scythe. Until it kept regenerating. While Judas distracted Delirium, Henry's consciousness cleared up, and he had a moment to think. He didn't want to die, not in that moment and not in that way. He lacked the strength and the tools to act upon that notion now that he was so close to death. It took too long for Judas to make a choice. Henry's lips and fingertips are painted blue when his heart finally stops beating, and his body goes limp. With his death, Delirium dies too.

"You were too fucking late!" Opal yells.

At that moment, she breaks free.

CHAPTER 24

Pearl moves easily in her hands. Together they dance against Judas, who intercepts the blows with his own. Third movement, cut short. Judas plays defense. She intercepts. Cycle of life, she spins Pearl using her own body as leverage. His eyes widen as she levitates higher into the space. The cyclone she got so accustomed to doing. She surges for him, relentlessly. He attempts to block, planting his blade forward, using it as a shield. Her whirling speed crashes onto him, forcing him to land on the ground with a CRACK! The realm fractures when he takes the impact of her attack.

She stands before him, towering above, while he lies on top of the cracked realm. To Era's entertainment, her arm moves Pearl's blade in the shape of a heart. She slices through the atmosphere, and in terror, he stills under the glowing heart. It beams with purifying light that effectively blinds him. He is bathed by the bright beam when he feels warmth for the first time after being dead for so long. His usual pessimism turns positive. His soul yearns for change so loudly that he is estranged as to how he wasn't able to hear it before.

"Hope?" He breathes out.

"He's dead because of you. If you hadn't stopped me, if you made up your stupid mind faster, he would still be alive!" She says, her brown bunching. Her face twisted in rage, and Judas couldn't help but think "Pretty" when he looked at her.

He sets his open hand in front of himself and his scythe, in hopes that she won't further his attack.

"Okay–okay, calm down." He says. Wrong words.

"Do not tell me to calm down! Era is right about us; we are slow and incompetent with our feelings."

"Sorry…What I want to say is that this case was different. You said it yourself, he was sick. Delirium was not an ordinary Rogue; it only dies when he does. Delirium developed secondary to his Dementia. Interfering would have likely extended his life, no doubt, and maybe interrupted his suffering momentarily, but it would have repeated itself sooner or later. I admit I was wrong and that it took me too long to make a decision, and for that I am sorry. If I had done so sooner, he might have had time to reconsider or allow someone to intervene." The warm light from Opal's bright heart shape continues to hug him.

"I don't want to be a coward anymore. I think you're right, subconsciously I always thought you were right, I was just afraid. I tried buying time so that maybe we could find a way to work things out, and I also wanted to see you again." He blushes at the admission and clears his throat. "The law is broken. I'm not entirely sure in what way, but I do understand that it's not right. All thanks to you."

Her grip on Pearl softens, steadily bringing her down. As she lowers her blade, the beaming heart begins to vanish.

"It didn't have to be this difficult for you to tell me what you actually think? So, now what?" She says.

"I'm sorry for Henry, Opal. I hope we can fight for his afterlife in the near future. While we build a persuading case to present to the Gods, I guess we run, and we fight until we get caught…together." Judas replies.

"You won't turn me in?" Their eyes meet and latch on to each other.

"I never really intended to, until recently, the Gods were starting to be pushy and questioned if I was your ally. At some point, I did think of joining you. With the Gods on my tail, I was hesitant to capture you because subconsciously, I understood you. The few times I helped you get away, I just wouldn't be at peace if you were harmed because of me, and to think I was going to do just that a little while ago. I truly hope you can forgive me. The Gods can try to capture us, but we won't go without a fight." He says, determination written all over his face.

"We would never beat them, Judas. Also, don't add this to your guilt list. I forgive you. We have plenty of souls to fight for, it is expected that we won't be able to free all of them." Opal runs her hands through her hair after she mounts Pearl on her back.

"Likely not, but we could try. And, thank you." Judas realizes he is still sitting on the cracked ground of Medio. He looked at Opal's new attire. He looks at her soft, wavy, long hair and the way her bangs part in the center. He admires the detail of the armor and the delicate embossing in her boots. "Pretty." He thinks again with a flush to his cheeks, but how could he blush with no blood?

"I'm glad you like it." Opal winks at Judas, thinking of Era, she was sure she was rolling over this moment while she watched it on her television.

Judas clears his throat. "By the way, my chest felt warm and fuzzy when that bright light covered me. What was that?"

"I'm not sure. It was the first time I tried using that movement." She covers her giggles with her hand.

"And you thought it would be a good idea to try it on me?! You could have killed me!" He places his hand with a wicked, sarcastic smile. All that was followed by their laughter, it was a melody so scarce and estranged to this realm.

"You're already dead." She continues laughing when she recalls what he said. "You said the word hope when it happened. What did you mean?"

"Well, it felt like my body told me everything was wrong and that it would all be okay at the same time. It was hope, I haven't felt it in a while, but I would never mistake it. I truly believe that light was the purest form of hope. I bet Rogues would love that." He holds his chin in thought for a few seconds.

Opal stands quietly, thinking about everything that just happened. Excitement grows in her when she thinks about fighting Rogues alongside Judas; she thought she could introduce him to Era. During her train of thought, she finally offers Judas a hand to help him off the cracked floor. A dim glow seeps through the fractures as he takes her hand to stand. There it is again, minuscule electric currents passing through their palmar embrace. Neither of them mentions that holding each other's hands felt right, like their hands were molded for each other. Together, they approach

Henry's body, intending to finish his cord-cutting when the realm begins to quake.

CHAPTER 25

The glowing cracks on the floor fracture into an all-encompassing rift. Two dozen Reapers hover through perfectly formed into two straight lines much like soldiers. The dimension of Medio is wide open, while this particular pocket is invaded by floating cloaks. Judas hastily holds Opal's arm, keeping her in place.

"What are you doing? We can still run." She whispers to him and, at the same time, tries to pull her arm free.

"No, we can't, there is something about the God's rift that is locking this pocket in place, I can feel it."

"You can feel that?" She asks skeptically.

"After doing this for so long, you start to notice certain things about Medio. Just play along, alright." She holds his eyes hostage for a second, and with that, she decides to trust him, although the lingering fear of betrayal sits in the back of her mind. She contemplates that maybe he'll bargain her for a better afterlife, or maybe he didn't care about her cause at all, and somehow this was all a ruse to capture her. To Opal, it seemed too convenient that he was professing his intentions to go Rogue, and then this happened at the same time. What if she's wrong? The opposite could be true. It was too late to run, and Pearl was not vibrating. Although the whole situation was going sideways, something about playing along with Judas felt right.

His attention moves back to the scene playing out in front of them. He risks a side glance her way. He notices that the bunch in her brow slackened, and she stood calm beneath his grip. He wanted to hug her in that moment. He could sense that she decided to trust him, and nothing could change how fluttered his chest felt in that moment for her. Opal, who was brave, kind, and selfless. The one who turned the afterlife upside down. The girl who helped him realize how wrong he was and the one who reminded him how to love.

"Love?" He thought. "I can't possibly be in love with her, I barely know her." He glances at her again, and the stomach-drop feeling is undeniable.

"Fuck, I am in love." He thinks to himself.

The Reapers stop spilling out of the rift. Judas snapped his attention back to the pressing matters. If he played this right, they shouldn't be separated. He clears his throat quietly and uses his most monotone voice. The same voice the Gods knew him by, and the voice Opal would not recognize, because with her, he stopped using that tone of voice after her first day of training with him.

"I have captured the fugitive," Judas announces.

He holds her in a tight grip, although gentle in nature, with currents still flowing between their touch. She looks above her and wonders if Era is watching the turn of events. Era, who is likely kicking her feet, watching the tense moment playout live on her television, all while eating grapes like popcorn.

Opal follows along just as Judas asked. She had to keep herself from spiraling into a storm of doubt. She wondered how he planned to help her, or if he was planning to help her at all. It was hard to read him with the stoic face he had drawn. The way his grip was not bruising, and the electric waves that ran through his fingertips, comforted her into fully trusting her.

"Opal, how could you trust him? You just met him." She thought to herself, and yet she did just that. She trusted him wholeheartedly.

Era lies on her back, effectively kicking her feet! Throwing grapes in the air as Judas and Opal stand together in front of her television. This was a tense moment and one that would likely not lead to a happy ending. She relished in the tension and the soft burn of their developing relationship.

"You so like him! Stop pretending like you don't!" She yells at the television, noticing the glances they occasionally send each other.

"Opal and Judas sitting by a tree, K-I-S-S-I-N-G!" She repeats over and over, laughing and rolling over her daybed.

As if in slow motion, they hover through the walkway the lined-up Reapers created and crossed straight into Cielo, specifically the Judgment chamber. The Reapers floated as usual with their heavy cloaks and hoods covering all traces of human emotions.

"I'm getting a judgment. They should get the same courtesy." She says loudly, hoping everyone, including the Gods, would hear. Little frowns poke through from underneath their hoods. She senses that Judas is biting back a smile or possibly a scold, when he squeezes her arm a few times.

The judgment chamber is the exact same, a courtroom holding a trial for someone already deemed guilty. The Gods sit on three distinct platforms in their respective thrones. In the center, well below them at the height of their shins, sits a small podium-type stand for the defendant. This time, the empty sides were not covered in stars and galaxies, but a spot for a Jury, a large Jury. Planet Earth decorates the area above the Gods its massive as if looking at it from a spaceship. Earth holds testament to the actions that will take place in this chamber, and with a blanket of glittering stars covering the rest of the space, it witnesses the trial.

"I am responsible for capturing the fugitive. I request to be assigned as her guard to ensure she does not escape again." Judas persuades in the direction of the God of the Underworld.

"Very well, ensure to keep that weapon out of her hands." Dannato commands.

Pearl quakes on her, the scythe likely equally nervous as Opal. Judas gently removes it from her back and, with care, places it on his own. The scythe is criss-crossed with his own. Opal risks yet another glance his way to search his face for any sign of betrayal or loyalty. She ponders what he requested, and his intentions dawn on her: he doesn't want them to be separated. Judas glances her way, seemingly unable to contain the need to look at her soft, heart-shaped face. Dannato has a small smirk on one side of his lips, seeming amused with something he noticed between the two.

"We still have matters to attend to. And, pending agreements before your judgment. You will wait in your quarters, accompanied by Judas, who will be held accountable if you escape." Parity says with her soft, feminine voice. She sits in the center so elegantly draped over to the side of of her throne with her legs crossed. Opal couldn't help but compare Era and Parity. They are both beautiful and out of Earth's beauty standards, but they were different kinds of beauty.

Parity is serene and harmonious. Era is a thunderstruck with high contrast. Parity soothes. Era taunts. Parity sits in a squeaky clean white throne with a matching outfit, where Era sits in an ornate mansion full of mixed-matched items sofisticatedly adorning a red velvet daybed.

"They're such opposites...Era's better." Opal thinks to herself, fully aware that she is biased toward her friend.

"Hold on. I also have plenty to say, starting with this..." Opal reaches into her steel corset.

"You do not have the right to speak here! After everything you have done, you dare ask to speak! Insolent little bra—"

"I didn't mean to you." Opal interrupts Deus's outburst.

"How dare you interrup–" His sentence is cut short with Dannato's raised hand.

"Speak quickly, we have matters to attend to." His smooth voice slither through her skin like the velvet on Era's daybed, forcing a chill to run through her body.

At this specific moment, she understood Era. His red eyes are carefully trained on her, and his jet black, perfectly straight hair frames his soft features as he takes a bite from an apple that rivals his eyes in color. Judas clears his throat softly, barely audible, which snaps Opal's staring contest with Dannato. The God of the Damned raises a brow at the sudden, yet subtle, demonstration of jealousy from Judas's part.

"Oh, right! I was instructed to give this to you." Opal tries to flatten the wrinkles out of the letter.

With the bend of a single finger, the letter floats to Dannato, somehow growing to the size of his massive hand when it arrives to him. Opal had forgotten that the Gods were enormous. Maybe Era was capable of growing, or they were capable of shrinking? Otherwise, their relationship would be... interesting.

"Who instructed you?" His brow raises, letter in hand. "I'm assuming whoever gave you that ensemble, it's in good taste, but we're not here to address that." He opens the letter only to close it quickly.

She could have sworn a brief flush of pink colored his cheeks just as he started coughing and clearing his throat. As if he's choking on something, and the room was suddenly too hot for him. He readjusts in his throne with one final clearing of his throat.

"Era, what on Earth did you send the man?" She shoots the question with a glare to the sky rather than words.

Meanwhile, Deus starts to huff and puff, wanting to make his shortening temper tantrum apparent. Parity only looks at Dannato, amused by his momentary loss of composure.

"Very well, be on your way." He instructs Judas to take Opal away to her Reaper quarter.

"You'll know when we need your presence." Parity says when they step off the stand and float down the path. Judas slices a rift open and leaves the higher powers to discuss Opal's future without her.

CHAPTER 26

"Make this the last time you shush me in front of mortals!"

"Must you always yell, Deus? How are you not exhausted by your own nuisance? Don't you ever tire from being such... a brute?" He bites his apple.

Dannato carefully folds the letter and tucks it in the plate of his charcoal armor. With his hand, he pats his pectoral a few time still captivated by the contents of the letter. He thinks of the possibilities that could arise from such a being.

"Gentlemen. We have matters to discuss. Please put a pause in your sword-measuring contest so that we can come to a conclusion once and for all. Now that we have the girl, we must all be on the same page immediately." Parity adds that, for once, she is becoming aggravated by Deus and Dannato's constant bickering. This whole situation is starting to remind her of a previous debate, and she feared that it could come to the same result..

I don't understand the issue. She is a criminal and deserves punishment, not special treatment, end of story." Deus folds his arms across his chest and tucks his delicate, feathered wing behind him.

"You're so stubborn and slow-witted." Dannato rubs his temples. "She does not deserve to be punished for something that is not entirely her fault; this whole situation is technically our fault. Opal demonstrated that our law is clearly flawed, and fixing it is the only option. I propose a reform." The haunting beauty of the God of the Underworld relaxes into his chair. He thinks of the contents of the letter, snaps his fingers, and a bushel of grapes appears instead of his usual apple.

"Oh come on, Dannato! A reform? Are you serious? I constructed this law and the Reaper division, and you expect me to just allow you to meddle with your stupid gloved hands in my business?"

"Our business, Deus!" Parity levels her stark white eyes at him, showing disapproval for his arrogance. She brushes her thin fingers through her silky white hair, ensuring that it's perfectly in its place. "You both have had a quarrel for the length of our eternity. Must I remind you what the first disagreement cost one of you?" She points her gaze at the golden feathers of Deus's single wing.

Outrage sprouts from the one-winged God with the memory of the first Deul thrown at him. Parity sits back in her spotless throne and waits for his tantrum to finish.

"We can always let her scale the steps of Purgatory while coming to a decision, or for eternity. I think it would be a fair compromise to allow her the opportunity to earn her way to Paradise. Although I am intrigued by a reform."

"I oppose it!" The God of Paradise arises from his seat.

"Deus, be quiet for a moment." She motions for him to sit. "Dannato, please elaborate." She continues.

"Thank you, mad'am. Brute–" He tips an imaginary hat at him as he takes the stand to present his proposal.

"It's a very simple process. But I'll explain it with numbers so that the less astute can understand." He winks at Deus and proceeds to pace in the center.

With a snap of his fingers, the podium where Opal stood expanded to one befitting a God. He leans on it slightly, throwing a single grape in his mouth. The popping sensation and the sweet nectar sent his head in ribbons for a movement. It was that moment that he made a decision regarding Era's letter. Another snap of his fingers, and he exchanges the grapes for an apple and focuses on the debate ahead.

"Keep snacking on fruits, King of the softies, clearly you don't have an actual argument or context for such an irrational proposition. Keep leaning back and looking pretty, I much prefer you that way." Deus says.

"Aww, you think I'm pretty?" Dannato responds tauntingly with his batting eyelashes. "Very well, let's begin." He smiles wickedly.

"First, we reinstate judgment for everyone, including suicide victims. Apparently, taking your own life does not make you a horrible person. By nullifying their judgment, we do not get an accurate picture of their intentions, the quality of their soul, and overall levels of virtue or evil. The current law is especially unfair to all current Reapers." Dannato begins to pace again.

"Second, we add a branch at the level of the Reapers, a warrior of some kind. If a person commits suicide, they will still serve one hundred years of service as either a Reaper or Warrior and then spend their eternity in their respective afterlife, where they deserve. We can discuss classifying criteria later."

"How do Reapers and Warriors differ?" Parity asks.

"A wonderful question, darling. Reapers collect souls after death and safely transport them to their final judgment. Warriors will have the opportunity to interfere with Rogues to an extent, of course. This new role would give humans the opportunity to reconsider and, therefore, get a second chance. Terms of the extent of interference can also be discussed later."

"It does sound promising and quite fair. Everyone gets the opportunity to be judged and have an adequate afterlife, one befitting of their actions. They will be sorted into their roles followed by their designated resting place." The Goddess of Purgatory ponders the proposal.

"I don't like it," Deus says, followed by the biggest eye roll the universe has seen coming from Dannato. "The previous law made things simple. Suicide is an insult to us, humans are ungrateful creatures. We grant them a gift to grow and prosper and be happy, and instead, they throw that gift right back at us. That does not deserve a reward!" Deus says through his teeth, biting down on the disdain he feels.

"Remember that Opal has shown us that suicide is not one-hundred percent, full stop, their fault. Yes, it was simple, but it was also not fair. The girl has presented an impressive argument. We are Gods, but we don't protect them. We sit on the sidelines as we watch them become infested with Rogues that coerce them to suicide and then punish them for it. We've never given them a fighting chance, we have failed as their creators. What part of that makes suicide a test? I argue that a better test is to see how they use a second chance, and if they turn their lives around with our protection, intervention, and hope. Even a fracture of it can be powerful." Dannato takes a crunching bite of his apple.

"And the other Reapers?" Deus retorts.

"Were you not listening? I said *everyone* gets a judgment." Dannato responds, exaggerating every syllable.

Parity watches both Dannato and Deus go back and forth with the proposition. She stands and heads over to Deus's throne and gracefully sits on the arm of his golden throne. She caresses one of the feathers in his wing. She senses their rivalry burning.

"I do agree with you, Dannato. In order for our Divine law to change, we all must agree. Deus–" she says to the golden God while she still admires his feathers, "promise to at least think about it during Opal's trial." She says like a purr.

"What am I witnessing here?" Dannato raises his brow. "Are you two..?"

"Not quite." Parity answers in a clipped tone.

The Goddess takes pride in being non-partisan when it comes to their disagreements, but always makes their position regarding the matter crystal clear. However, Parity might have been the one to help Deus recover from their previous Deul. Gods heal quickly, and they are immortal, but that doesn't mean they don't feel pain.

"Fine. I'll think about it. I make no promises, and I want it known that I still do not agree." He unfolds his arms and leans back in his seat, only slightly pouting and trying not to enjoy how the Goddess admires his wing.

"Bring her in." Parity commands.

CHAPTER 27

Her chamber looks just how she had left it. Her tallies still decorate the walls of the room. The bench is in the same position, and her thick blanket is neatly folded at the foot of it. Judas and Opal sit on the bench with their shoulders slightly brushing against each other. Both noting the contact and neither retreat. A moment passes and then another. There is no way of knowing how long it will take the Gods to finish their discussion. They relish in the quiet peace, not daring to break the tension with their words.

"I understand what you were trying to do," Opal says.

Between her fate in the Gods' hands and this specific moment, she was not sure what made her more nervous. Judas makes her feel uneasy and yet completely unafraid. He is the one constant thing in this pandemonium, alongside Pearl and now Era, that has kept her from losing all hope. On Earth, she would have pondered the idea of asking him out on a date or drinking some coffee together. It is too bad there are no such things in this place, maybe in Paradise, but it was hard to imagine how Deus managed that place.

She wanted to converse and explore his mind. There was not enough time in the present for all the questions she wanted to ask him everything, and learn all the details of his life. She understands that he carries immense guilt, unresolved feelings, and unexplored grief. There is the possibility that he does not understand that himself or is simply running away from self-forgiveness. He had helped her despite his own questions; he led her into the unknown and still held her hand. Opal wanted to hold his hand so badly, but with the current state of their fate, she wasn't sure it was wise.

"I'm glad." He purses his lips.

An awkward silence sits between them, with an odd tension filling the space. The scenes of what had happened played in her head. The multiple times he helped her and her need to tell him what she feels. Opal never liked the taste of regret.

"I can't be in love with her." He kept repeating to himself since the last realization. "You just met her, and you're both dead." He brushes his fingers through the top portion of his hair.

"We might have still had a chance to run away. We could have had more time." She says.

"We couldn't, like I said in the moment, the pocket of Medio was locked there was no way to open another rift, and there is no point in delaying the inevitable. I was about to become your accomplice and a fellow fugitive. If we were caught under different circumstances, we would certainly be separated. You would stand on that podium alone, and I can't stand the thought of that. I promise, you will not be alone at the stand. I will be by your side until the very end or until I am removed by force."

One look at the warmth in her eyes, and his heart was molten lava. God did he wish he could take her hand in marriage and hand her father twenty goats in exchange. They only knew each other for such a short time, but the life expectancy of humans was lower when he was alive. It was not uncommon for marriages to happen faster or arranged.

"What are you thinking? She's from the modern world. Her father would likely prefer cows or lumber." He thinks to himself.

Her soft, heart-shaped face and lovely curtain bangs frame her small, almond-shaped eyes so well that they held him captive. It was strange to remember how to feel human feelings, but with the lovely ones also came the ones he tried so hard to bury deep and forget. He clears his throat, breaking their staring contests.

"By the way, I meant to tell you earlier, but the Gods have asked Reapers to Jury the judgment. The subject of fairness is on the table since you are the first Reaper to ever gain judgment."

"You really don't think I deserve it, huh?"

"I think you deserve it, I'm sure others do too, but I also believe some of us deserve our current sentence." He looks at her again. During his response, she must have moved closer because his nose is now a few centimeters away from hers. They both could not resist dipping their gaze at each other's lips.

"Shit! I do like him." She finally accepts the reality of her longing for Judas. In such a short time, he of all people reached for her heart in death and somehow managed to catch it.

"You deserve it too." She says.

It was hard to comprehend what was happening between them. In the center of chaos, love and the power of attraction managed to grow out of nothing. It dawned on her the cruelty of finding your person without time to get to know each other and fall in love. Time was not a luxury they had, as both their fates hung in different hands.

"Out of all of us Reapers, I can tell you for a fact that I deserve this sentence." His lids close over his eyes tightly. He suppresses the need to tell her everything that he feels. But Judas doesn't want to burden her heart with that, especially now when they could make better use of their likely last moments together.

He startles when Opal's hand brushes against his cheek and holds his face so close to her. He indulges in the contact of her hand and the sight of her brown colored eyes.

"I think you deserve justice. You also deserve forgiveness, not from others but from yourself."

"How could I forgive myself?" Judas sits, overwhelmed by all his suppressed emotions resurfacing.

He stood on the precipice of a cliff next to her, and he fell. Judas free-falls not into an open body of water, instead he falls straight into her arms. He melts under her tight embrace and gives himself permission to feel.

"I'm pathetic, I know." He scolds himself.

In his time alive, he would have been stoned for showing such weakness. There was only one man who would not have scolded him for crying and showing emotions. His friend, his teacher, would have been the arms to console him from the world. The one who would break bread with him and wash his feet without pride or prejudice. He would have helped him navigate the complexities of being human, and he is the one he felt the most guilty for.

His eyes are dry still because how could he cry after inflicting so much pain on someone? How could he play the victim when he was the villain in someone else's story? After so much time running away and pretending a cloak and a hood would eternally justify his self-deprecation, it was time he faced the scariest confrontation of all: himself. Defying the odds, his eyes dampen, and those tears he stored like water in drought finally rained from his eyes.

"Would he have forgiven you?" Her words are sharp and delicate.

His face rests in her palm, and so does his heart in that moment. And with a brutally gentle awakening to the realization that his friend, his teacher, did, in fact, forgive him. He was the one who was consumed by guilt after his friend's death. He blamed himself for his treason and took responsibility for the tragedy. The man was of the purest hearts and a leader who condoned leading with love and compassion. He advocated for the marginalized and for forgiveness. He was love, and he was hope. He was already forgiven.

Judas was the one holding the rope around his own neck. It only took some whispering in his ears.

"Murderer...Murderer...Murderer..."

"You did this!"

"Monster!"

"What did those gold coins get you? Was it worth it?"

"Do it...Do it...Do it..."

"Jump. Jump. JUMP!"

And, a push to his legs. A pounding feeling in his chest and endless poking to his head for him to jump and hang off the branches of a Redbud tree.

Never in his long afterlife did Judas think that a woman with too much empathy in her heart and nothing to lose would help him realize that. She would be the reason for change and justice in this place.

"He did forgive me. I just couldn't." A small sob breaks from him.

Her other hand holds the other side of his face, and her eyes peered into his. She peered into the windows of his soul that held so many caged feelings, finally free from their shackles. Without knowing what else to look for, there they both sit and admire the growth of their souls. A few minutes pass, his sobbing softens, and his tears dry. The only thing left is an ache in his chest, not from a heart, but from the evidence that his soul once belonged to a person who owned one. Judas relishes the feeling, and in that moment, he wanted to show Opal how truly grateful he was for this moment and for her.

Opal realizes she has been holding his face a long time, too long for friends. She wanted to keep holding him. The sounds of his sobs broke her, and she wanted to do anything that would make him feel better. Alas, she lets go of his face. She sits back. Judas watches her with terror, a little alarm rings in his head as the panic of her far proximity consumes him.

Without thinking, just like every time they saw eachother, he reaches for the delicate strands of her hair. The strands that he has admired so many times. She tracks every movement he makes, her chest flutters even without a physical heart.

"Opal...May I?" He asks.

Their faces stood so close, enough to notice the small specks of black in her eyes. The smile lines in his face were obscured by those of the frown that he carried for so long. Her prominent cheekbones. His long and dark lashes. At some point, their foreheads ended up resting on each other, feeling the magnetic force that pulled them together.

"You may." She responds.

In that instant, his lips gently encase hers. He has never indulged in something so lovely. Their lips dance to the rhythm of a slow waltz with deliberate and tender movements. Showing eachother what words could not convey. In this moment, two tormented souls joined together in comfort in the most natural human emotion: love.

Her mouth welcomed the soft pressure of his lips, and she allowed herself to feel everything. Their souls understood each other. They had no physical life, and somehow, she was finally living. His hands traveled to the sides of her face, holding her together while their worlds collided. A moment she wished would never end.

After a while, they broke off from the kiss, only for him to tightly embrace her again, this time with his arms. It had been so long since he felt the intimacy of a hug, a genuine human connection. They sat on the bench, hugging each other, waiting for fate to work itself out. The red clock began a countdown starting at five minutes.

"They want us back in five minutes." Opal says muffled through their embrace.

He shushes her.

"We have five minutes to enjoy possibly the last hug we will ever get." He says while his hands softly brush through the wavy strands of her hair.

"He's right." She thought.

They don't know what awaits them beyond the chamber, so they relish the comfort the present has gifted them instead.

The clock strikes time, and he escorts her back to the chamber. He transforms into an immovable tree planted at her side the second they arrive at the podium. Dannato's brow raises at the gesture and notices the different energy between them.

Rows of hooded Reapers fill the seats of the Jury, stilling in the presence of giants. There were so many of them that she wondered if they were all there or just a few.

"Opal Tempest, welcome to your first and final judgment. This is the first time we have ever had the pleasure of doing this with a Reaper and also a Jury." Parity tilts her head forward in acknowledgement of the endless rows of hooded Reapers and sharp, glistening scythes. "Collectively, we have decided that your case is unique, and after countless debates regarding your defiance, the weight of your actions, and more importantly, the weight of your soul." She sits as a swan would, finely floating on serene waters.

Her gown is so simple with delicate ruffles at the hem. Her face shows a calm demeanor and a semblance of confidence.

"Your actions have shed light on the nature of our laws regarding suicide, Rogues, and the fairness of our judgment laws." Dannato follows with the crunch of an apple.

The Gods list her actions on Earth, her actions in the afterlife, and place them on a theoretical balance. Some are light as a feather, some the weight of bricks. They described the times she may have insulted someone, self-degradation, hit and runs, accidental theft, and any small negative gesture is taken into account. The time she helped an old lady across the street, when she stood up for the kid being bullied at school, the times she bought homeless people food, the time she gave her little brother her ice cream because he dropped his, and any other positive action she performed. She was being dissected in front of everyone. They looked at the most intimate aspects of her life, and they described in vivid detail how she killed herself.

Her moral compass was discussed and debated. She was questioned by the Gods individually. And for a few minutes, the whole Jury left to discuss her fate without the Gods. They dispersed in someone's Reaping chamber, they had organized a discussion. The Jury of the Gods waived their solitude for the day, and they gained access to interaction.

"We deserve judgment. I was a good person. I don't even remember how I killed myself." One Reaper says.

"Opal Tempest did break the rules. At first, I didn't agree, but I understand now. I saw what happened with the little boy Erik with my own eyes. Her interference saved so many lives." Another adds.

"How did I never connect the dots? Rogues have such a large influence on our lives. Suicide, for the most part, is not autonomous, but we are punished as if it were, and even so, that alone does not dictate the kind of person I was." A Reaper in the front, leading the discussion, says.

"She broke the law, but the law is already broken. She is innocent." The Reaper adds.

"She's innocent!" They all say in unison.

All Reapers reappear in the chamber. The energy between the three Gods is tense, they were in disagreement, and Opal could see it. Parity stood to voice the verdict when Deus stopped the ritual. He stands next to Parity and whispers something in her ear.

"Parity, I still have some questions to address with her. Could you please sit down or stand by while I ask them?" A question in such a soft tone was out of character for the golden angel. She looks at him with a sharp eye and sits back down on her throne with a bitter taste in her mouth. Dannato and Parity look at each other, slightly shaking their heads.

"Miss Tempest, considering that you are being granted a courtesy that none of the other have, I wonder what makes you so deserving?" Deus gestures towards the Jury.

The feeling of a thousand pairs of eyes burns into her side profile. This was her moment to advocate for them. This was the moment she could make the biggest impact in the name of real change. The trial was focused on her and her fate, solemnly taking the others into account. It was odd since the Gods had brought the Reapers to witness.

"They are as deserving as I am, if not more. Taking our lives was not entirely our fault, and even then, one action does not dictate the weight of my entire life. As we know, there is an outside force punching and coercing us to commit suicide. But, there are cases like Henry's, where a Rogue manifests from an illness, and it's unavoidable. Henry is the prime example of how Suicide doesn't automatically make you worthy of eternal suffering in the Underworld. I didn't realize this until I re-lived my own death. In those last moment my mind was not my own, it was blank, and the only thoughts were those planted there by those haunting voices. I was pushed to do this. Yes, I take responsibility for all the actions that led me to that moment, but I do not take responsibility for being manipulated, and neither should the rest of you!" Opal amplifies her voice so everyone can hear her loud and clear.

"Interesting." Dannato rubs his jaw. "I have something to add." He adds.

"Opal, is it? I had made a proposal to my colleagues about a reform in our law regarding suicide. How would you feel about such a change?" His bright red eye peer in to her soul.

"It all depends on how you change it? If you change some-thing unfair to something similar, then there is no change. But, if you really change it for the good, then I think it is the only right thing to do." She says with her chest out and chin forward.

"Jury!" Parity stands not giving the golden God another chance to interrupt. " Those in favor of the Opal Tempest's innocence and in favor of a reformation, please raise your scythes." She announces.

A hymn resounds in the space, similar to those you would hear in a Gregorian temple. One by one, the scythes are raised into the air in solidarity. Dannato and Parity sit back, relinquishing the moment. Meanwhile, Deus's forehead vein is about to create a fault line on Earth.

Opal watches the scene in awe of the support. With an overwhelming sense of support and gratification that she did something good. She felt the souls of the Reapers reaching for her with their voices, longing for the change that she has been fighting for.

"I, too, stand with Opal. I, too, stand for a reform." Judas announces and takes her hands. "You are supposed to protect us. Why are we blamed for the lack of it?"

Their hands grip tight whilst the melody emanating from the Jury earns the sky a single diamond speck. A new star is born from the newly found hope of those who are deceased and unjustly damned. Haunting and beautiful, their voices sing, stabbing a sharp blade of years of discontent, pain, and injustice into the chest of the three mighty Gods.

"I refuse to Reap without justice!" Judas shouts.

KLANK!

He drops his scythe onto the ground.

"I will not Reap without judgment!" He shouts again, followed by a wave of similar sounds riding through the rows of Reapers in the Jury. The same Reapers who now chant the words Judas declared onto the Gods.

"We will not Reap without justice. We will not Reap without judgment!"

These words resounded in the chamber over and over. The Reapers chant their new law, established by themselves. While two out of three of the Gods stand moved by the display of valor, one God sits disgusted by the defiance.

Chapter 28

"The insolence of this one has incited a revolt! Such defiance must be punished!"

"Deus, you know that's not the reason they revolt. In fact, they aren't revolting at all; they simply ask for justice." Parity says tenderhearted. She could feel their sorrow through their chants, she could feel the imbalance in the universe. She felt it for a while, but dismissed it, it was not often a Goddess felt guilty.

The Gods created Earth with a feather from Deus, a hair strand from Dannato, and a single exhale from Parity. They meticulously molded it until it was up to their standards. Through evolution, humans developed, and along side them, multiple forms of life. The current divine law was established by the three with their newfound arrogance as deities. They were excessively proud of their creation's ability to sustain life, and as a gift, they decorated the skies with constellations, the grass with flowers, and fields with fruits. After years of looking after Earth, it took one person's suicide in the early stages of human evolution for the first Rogue's birth.

Initially, Rogues were not an issue. There were a few of them, and they were more like a small pest, a nuisance. As time progressed, they learned how to multiply and that with numbers they held power through persuasion. They learned how to manifest on Earth and who their best targets were. With their presence, the third realm created itself and expanded so large that souls started getting lost after death. They became stuck in uncharted territory and required guidance, which was an issue since the Gods were unable to enter the realm.

Deus had suggested the law and the creation of the Reapers, he is indeed the founder. He considered human life sacred and humans weak for bending to Rogue influence. The golden angel also considered humans the perpetrators of this whole situation since Rogues were born of human nature. In his eyes, humans who committed suicide were undeserving and responsible for the creation of Rogues. As time went on, life on Earth evolved and became so complicated by the day. Medio kept growing, and since it was adjacent to Earth, it was easy to infect and also served as a barrier between realms. Souls were increasingly lost in Medio, and a solution was needed as soon as possible. This happened for years until Dannato and Parity finally agreed to think about Deus's proposition.

Medio now rivaled the size of the two realms. It was possibly larger since it had pockets within itself. Multiple times, the Gods attempted interventions and failed miserably, eventually they all agreed to Deus's proposal. The Reapers were an official unit and momentarily solved the issue, until now.

"The law is absolute! They do not deserve judgment. Your stupid reform proposition is unacceptable. Without suicides, there wouldn't be Rogues in the first place. They are responsible for the chaos in Medio, which means that their sentence is fair! It's their fault!" Deus slams his hand onto the arm of his shiny throne.

"I disagree. The time when we established that law was different, and it seemed like the best option at the time. I no longer think this is fair. Their lives are so complex now, and Rogues infect their minds, their bodies, and their realm, unchecked. There is no order or justice. What a disgrace that we have allowed this issue to brew for this long. If we had interfered sooner, we wouldn't have positioned ourselves in this predicament now." Dannato inspects an apple in his hand while speaking.

"I have to agree with Dannato, Deus. Without balance, there is no justice." Parity throws her words at the God of Paradise, and they take a moment to look at each other as if they are having a silent conversation amongst themselves.

"Oh, for the love of everything written! What is going on between you two?" Dannato shouts, noticing the clear tensions.

"Nothing!" They both respond at the same time.

Parity looks away with her usual calm demeanor returning. Deus continues to argue with Dannato, tensions rising, and with that, their volume. They yell at each other, both stand with their faces tilted above Parity, who sits leaningback and observing their dramatic display.

"You are an incompetent God! Can't you see this—this human wants to manipulate us. We are the ones with power, not her." Deus says.

"I've had enough of your arrogance. You are insufferable. It will never amaze me how you, out of all beings came to be a God! Are you unable to see through their eyes, feel through their souls, and put yourself into their shoes? They already suffer so much on Earth with those things constantly whispering in their ears, and then what? They come to us, and we also turn our backs on them?" Dannato's cool semblance is enraged; his eyes shine ruby red as two flames consume the anger coursing through his body.

"No, I cannot, because I am not one of them! I think we have had enough of a discussion. It's time we attempt a different approach to assert this matter." Deus mirrors Dannato, the tension in his body allows ripples of corded golden muscle to tense in his arms.

Parity is still sitting under the solid bridge they created above her, slightly slouched on her throne while rolling her eyes at the argument. Deus's statement forces her to sit up. This was the moment she was hoping wouldn't come. This was the situation she was hoping they could avoid. She looks at Deus and then his wings, getting the sense that things are about to escalate.

"You wouldn't? This doesn't call for it." The Goddess rubs her temple, followed by a sigh. Deus glances at her, and his eye contact seems to hold an apology that changed really fast when his emerald green eyes turn their focus on the bright red ones across from him.

"I declare a Duel." The golden God extends his arm with an open palm, waiting for an acceptance of the challenge.

There has only been one Duel in their history over who would be appointed to rule specific domains of the afterlife. All Gods must agree on all disputes, and Duels are a simple solution when they are not able to come to terms with a decision. Parity does not take sides, her purpose is to ensure balance and fairness in their realm. Although her vote counts, all three must agree for a reform or new laws to be made.

His long black cape flows tractably behind the God of the Underworld. The crown on his head glimmers with grandeur as his arm extends forward, effectively cutting the tight tension between them to meet his hand in agreement.

Opal, Judas, and the Jury all stand in witness of the commencement of the second Duel. The moment their hands met, Opal swore the realm shook beneath them.

"I hope you remember how the last duel ended." Dannato laughs when he nods his head in the direction of Deus's beautiful golden feathered wing.

CHAPTER 29

The judgment chamber transforms with a quake into a place worthy of an epic battle. From a room full of podiums, stands, and Jury seats, to an enormous Colosseum with an ominous dirt arena in the center. The structure resembled the one on Earth, in Rome, but this was made of grey stone with large, worn-down ridges eating at the walls. The sky above them was still the glittering cosmos with Earth as their Sun. Small galaxies fill the eternal darkness, creating a jaw-dropping, colorful array of specks and sparkles.

Judas and Opal stand next to Parity, holding on to each other as the ground beneath them shakes in transformation. They stood at the center of the spectating area, which was traditionally where an Emperor would sit and observe a gladiator fight. The long rows of the rotunda were filled with seats occupied by the Reapers who were present as Jurors. Endless rows of hooded Reapers silently floating in their place.

"This is the second Duel to ever ensue between Gods. It never crossed my mind that this would happen again, at least not this soon. These two never stop bickering, which goes to show that even Gods can have serious disputes amongst us." Parity speaks to the crowd at the edge of the balcony. "There are three very simple rules." Her voice, powerful and amplified. She moves her arms with each phrase and animates herself as any good host would do.

"First, the Gods will not be allowed to use their powers or special abilities, such as flying. However, strength and brute force are allowed. Second, they each must choose one weapon and one weapon only; nothing else is permitted. Third, the battle ends when one yields or becomes unconscious, we are immortal after all." She chuckles after her own joke.

"Now, although we all know who our champions are, it is customary for them to introduce themselves and pledge their oath." Parity opens and raises her arms wide, signaling for the heavy metal gates to rise and reveal the Gods who are now champions.

The gate on the right reels up with loud clanking of metal chains, sending sound waves all around the Colosseum. The sidelines, on the other hand, are not as one would expect a Duel to have; the crowd did not roar or cheer, the Reapers floated silently as usual.

A tall, bulky figure emerges from the shadow. Corded muscle, a fully exposed torso, a simple knee-length loincloth, and a pair of brown leather gladiator sandals. His beautiful golden wing is tightly tucked behind him, and the gold in his feathers twinkles with the starlight reflecting off of them. His gold skin glimmers against the dark sky. If he weren't so cruel, he could be the sun in a solar system. His strong brow bone and squared jaw are concentrated with rage and pride. He strides towards the center, kicking dust up from the ground.

"Boo! Boo! Tomato! Tomato!" Opal yells loudly. She yells by herself; no one dares to join her chants. Judas admires her foolish courage with astonishment.

To the left, the chains sing with his entrance, and the shadows adjust to his movements. The clang of the metal cheers along every step he takes. His beauty is ethereal as his stirring beauty comes to the light. Opal continues to understand Era's feelings every time she sees him in a new light. Dannato opted for a more practical garment, although not traditional like Deus's loincloth, it's not forbidden. His torso is completely bare and on full display. Showcasing his broad shoulders, chiseled abdominal muscles, and carved pectorals. He's muscular yet not bulky, but athletic. He wore black parachute pants and matching leather combat boots. His hair is tucked behind him in a loose bun, and only a few strands perfectly frame his face. His red eyes promise pain to his opponent and justice to the realm.

The two champions approach the weapons rack. Deus's hand immediately snatches a large silver axe. Large. Sharp. Heavy. He swings it a few times, testing the feel of the handle in his hand and the weight of the blade with each movement. In his hand, it seems like it weighs nearly nothing. Holding the axe in place, he has made his choice.

Dannato palms a simple Onyx sword with silver embossing around the hilt, he doesn't bother to inspect or test it. The rack vanishes once their selections are confirmed. All that is left is a few pleasantries and a grueling battle ahead. A battle that will determine the fate of the afterlife.

"Champions recite your oath." Parity commands loudly.

It took a moment for Opal to notice Parity's change in apparel as well. She stood taller than both her and Judas. Opal was relieved to know that the Gods were indeed able to manipulate their sizes for Era's sake. Her gown was that same stark white made of sheer white fabric, perfectly falling off her left shoulder and delicately framing her bosom. Her hair is braided into rows of white braids stacked around the top of her head like a crown, and amongst them were bushels of angel's breath flowers, accentuating the halo that hovered above her head.

"I Deus, God of Paradise, solemnly swear to abide by all rules and fully bow to the outcome of the battle." His voice was steady and concentrated, unlike the loud and obnoxious demeanor he held in the judgment chamber.

"I, Dannato, God of the Underworld, solemnly swear to abide by all the rules and fully bow to the outcome of the battle." His tone was amused by the events about to take place, and a mischievous smile spreads his lips into a grin.

They both take a stance. Deus tenses his muscles and crouches in a Greek wrestling style with his axe in hand. Dannato stood straight up and relaxed holdin his blade at his side.

"Begin!" Parity announces into the rotunda of the Colosseum.

Without hesitation, Deus storms at full speed while Dannato readies for impact. The dirt under his leather sandals lifts into small clouds of dust following his movements. His axe cuts to the left and then to the right. His hands and feet were relentless with the inertia of his fighting. Dannato patiently avoids impact blocking with his blade. Sweat beads off Deus's forehead as he continues steadily. The large sloped blade of the axe oscillates, ebbs, and flows in different configurations with his knees, elbows, and fists. Move after move, he finally lands a blow.

"Eat dirt, princess" Deus shouts.

His elbow hits home in Dannato's abdomen, sending him flying across the arena. He collides into the wall, crumbling the stone at his back. A nimbus of brown dirt puffs into the area around him as he collapses onto the ground. A deafening silence awaits as the cloud clears. Deus also stands in defense, his form slackening by the minute, already accepting his victory. He drops the axe and extends his wing in attempts to rally up the stoic audience for applause. The audience stays unmoved, with the exception of one person.

"Boo! Boo! Tomato! Tomato! Get up, Dannato! Come on!" Opal yells over and over, jumping up and down. Deus spears a death glare in her direction and then turns to ignore her.

"That was easy enough, the prick had it coming." He says, turning his back once again. The crumbled wall is clear, and Dannato is nowhere in sight.

"Brute–" Deus chills at the sound of his silky voice.

Dannato stands, leaning against the opposite wall. With only a small cut on his lip and mirth at his opponent's demonstrations. At last a loud roar emanates from the crowd. Endless cheering for the Ruler of the damned. It was the first time the Reapers had shown any form of enthusiasm since the previous interactions in Opal's trial.

"Woohoo! Let's Go!" Opal jumps in place, clapping and cheering.

"That's pretty embarrassing for you." Dannato chuckles. "Surely you didn't think you won already? Such an arrogant fool!" His smooth laugh caresses the ears of everyone that watches intently.

Deus again advances first. Dannato accompanies him with a surge, giving up his defensive approach. Their blades touch and spark when they collide. Together they dance a deadly cavort.

CHAPTER 30

"Era, I hope you're watching this!" Opal says to the sky.

She stands between Judas and Parity watching the match, just as hypnotized as everyone around them. The fighting style of the two giants is surreal as if it were straight out of a movie. Their power is astonishing, they are fast and strong. Their movements are precise and calculated.

Deus is aggressive, unabated, and extremely strong. He aims for most possible damage without hesitation or second thought. He attempts to slice through joints and weak points. His axe looks just as heavy as he is, powerful with each slice of the blade. His weapon begged for contact with skin, and so did the rage in his bright green eyes. His tunic surprisingly stays in place and is no longer white but painted with streaks of blood and dirt.

On the other hand, Dannato is quick, wickedly skilled, and calculated. His patience is his biggest virtue when he analyzes his opponent for weakness, mistakes, and an opportunity to land an agonizing strike. He played defense for a while and learned Deus's combinations and body language. His pale skin now glimmered just as much as Deus's gold skin with the sheen of his sweat coating his muscles. The fight seemed to have no end as they watched from the safety of the balcony.

"Who won the last duel?" Judas asks Parity, interrupting their stunned silence as they witness the most epic battle the universe has witnessed for millennia.

Parity does not spare Judas a glance, her eyes remain focused on the battle as she acts as the referee and ensures all rules are followed.

"It is not typical for me to tell mortals our history, but considering you both are huge reasons why this is happening in the first place, I don't think it would be imprudent to divulge the story." Her eyes roam the two champions, landing on Deus and tracking his moves. A mixture of emotions trails her face: sadness, amusement, contempt, and perhaps attraction? "Have you ever wondered why Deus only has one wing?" She smirks, keeping her eyes glued to the arena.

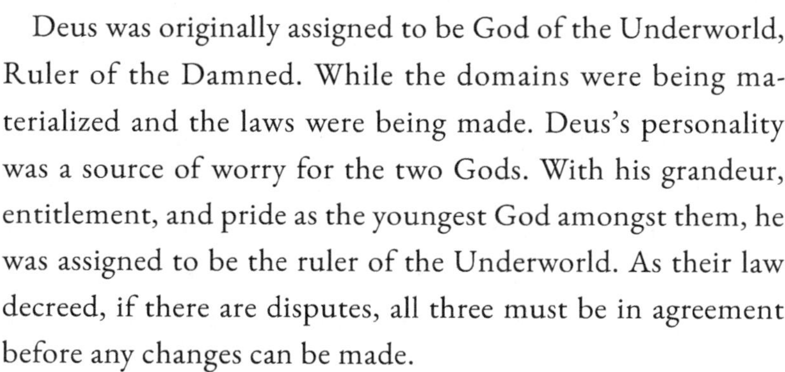

Deus was originally assigned to be God of the Underworld, Ruler of the Damned. While the domains were being materialized and the laws were being made. Deus's personality was a source of worry for the two Gods. With his grandeur, entitlement, and pride as the youngest God amongst them, he was assigned to be the ruler of the Underworld. As their law decreed, if there are disputes, all three must be in agreement before any changes can be made.

Dannato did not share the sentiment and thought assigning Deus to the Underworld was a mistake. He believed that punishment required equity and balance, that torment had to match the level of evil and sin in a person. When he opposed the decision, Deus believed himself the rightful ruler of that domain. Through discussion and debate, they attempted to reach a more diplomatic agreement. However, similar to Opal's situation, tensions grew, rivalry rose, and Deus's short-tempered nature snapped.

"You would be perfect with the goody-two-shoes upstairs, Dannato. Your soft and weakling heart has no business in the Underworld. I wouldn't want you to suffer while watching your poor little humans being tortured." Deus had said.

"Your arrogance and lack of empathy have no place in the Underworld. Punishment requires fairness and proper classification. I do not trust you to be fair in your torment." Dannato replied.

After countless debates, they still did not see eye to eye. Deus finally challenged Dannato to a Duel over the rule of the Underworld. Almost identical to the current, and a great example of what had happened before. Except that in the current Duel, their experience and power are better matched. In the first, Dannato was significantly more powerful than Deus because, although their birth or coming into existence is unknown, it is well-recognized that Dannato is the eldest amongst the three, followed by Parity and lastly Deus. Their lore is kept between them and whoever or whatever created them. Who is their creator? Do they even have one? A question no human or Reaper knows the answer to.

"In the end, Dannato cut off one of his wings, the unbearable pain left Deus collapsed and unconscious, resulting in his defeat. After Deus lost, he was officially crowned the God of Paradise." Parity concludes her brief history lesson.

A short-lived memory of Deus's bloody wing stub enters her mind as she watches the arena. Parity remembers leaving her home in the center of Purgatory, amongst the endless moving ladders and staircases onto different levels to visit the Golden angel in his cloud-like home in the heavens.He was sprawled across a throne made of clouds, on his belly, streaking his seat in a startling contrast of white and blood red. His stump was healing, although too slowly for pain to subside, he was still young and did not heal as fast as she or Dannato. She felt bad for him and attended to him until he regained strength. Since then, she occasionally visits him, where they speak about matters, and where she usually helps him soften his temper. Amongst them, a friendship formed, one that Dannato was not fully aware of.

"Will it grow back?" She had asked Deus.

"I have to earn them back." He responded.

It had been millennia since that battle, and she wondered what he had to do to earn his wings back. What had he done to not be worthy of growing the lost wing?

"Do you think history will repeat itself?" Judas asks, ripping her from her memory.

"For the sake of keeping the balance, I cannot say." Her words are clipped as she keeps focus on every blow and every move the Champion Gods make.

Occasionally, Judas spares a glance at Opal. He has been doing that the whole match, trying his best to avoid flashbacks of the last moment they had together in her chamber. She is fully immersed in the battle. She cheers for Dannato and chants disgraces at Deus. Her eyes are lit with enjoyment over the spectacle. Judas can't help the warm-like feeling that spreads through his chest, tugging up at the corners of his lips. He watches her unmeasured excitement, fully hypnotized by her. Unlike the rest of the crowd, his eyes could not leave her profile, and he found it hard to watch the battle at all.

CHAPTER 31

Puddles of blood and sweat scatter all over the dirt. Both champions stand face to face at the mercy of the other. Time is not the enemy, but it's also not their friend because the longer either of them takes to defeat their opponent, the more they exhaust themselves, lowering their chances of victory. The arena stands but holds all kinds of damage; the walls around the two are crumbled and cracked. They circle each other and break between punches. One spits blood, and the next round, the other follows.

Deus dives onto one knee, his axe follows his line of sight, attempting to ram it across Dannato's chest. The God of the Underworld realizes and somersaults, avoiding impact with the blade. The golden angel bloodies his shins as he slides through the rocky dirt, only to miss; he doesn't give up. From his knees he uses the momentum of his weight to impale forward with his axe. Dannato does the same with his sword. Both Champions begin to show signs of fatigue. Their maneuvers steadily become sloppy and desperate.

"Give up already!" Deus swings the axe to the right.

"You won't win this time." He swings an elbow across Dannato's face without hitting his mark. Instead, his nose meets Dannato's palm with a resonating, crunching sound.

Deus wipes the blood from his nose and gets back on his feet, out of breath. Streaks of dirt and mud were made from the mix of his sweat. Dannato mirrors his semblance, looking dirty and tired, with his parachute pants torn and his hair no longer in a neat bun.

"I do not yield. You, out of anyone in this place, should know better than to foolishly think I would ever surrender to a brainless Brute. I'll fight until the end." This time, Dannato initiates the contact and forges ahead towards Deus.

His arm tucked close with the sword, aiming for a final blow. His blade aims for the golden God's chest. Twice, slice to the right. Thrust to the left. Vertical chop. Multiple hits land but do not topple over the winged giant. He staggers one move after another until a bright idea enters his mind.

He uses his sword just like a certain Reaper would use her scythe. He is the eye of the storm as he spins at a constantly increasing speed. Unlike Opal, he does not levitate but spins like a tornado made of sharp cutting winds.

"Circle of Life," Dannato says.

"Holy shit!" Opal jumps up and down, pulling at Judas's sleeve. "He's using my move!" She claps and cheers with excitement. Judas fights for his balance as she pulls and tugs at him to watch.

Deus stands with his feet wide and sturdy, readying himself for the impact. There is no point in running or hiding. They both watched Opal use this attack a few times before she went off the grip, and every time it was useless for the Rogues to run. Her blade propelled her at an unnatural speed. Dannato's straight blade did the same. He rips through the space towards Deus at the center of a cyclone, barreling towards victory.

Opal blinks; he hits impact. A thick cloud of dust covers the outcome, but the sound of metal breaking echoes through the Colosseum. As the dust clears, it is visible that in the center, both Gods stand holding two shattered blades. Immediately, Deus lunges forward and begins to grapple with a snare. Dog fight. Cradle. He moved like a Greek Wrestler. His frame is large and his limbs are overbearingly strong. Physically, he might be more powerful than Dannato.

"Come on, Dannato! Get out from under him!" Opal yells as the crowd cheers.

This battle has now come down to brute strength. In that department, Deus had the fight won. The Ruler of the Damned has agility and speed. That has to be enough, right? The golden angel tightly tucks his opponent in an arm triangle choke. Leaving Dannato to smell the sweat of his wing. With the immense pressure, Dannato could feel his consciousness inching towards a peaceful blanket of tranquility and rest.

"You smell like a dog!" Dannato yells at Deus.

"As if you smell like roses?" Deus says not letting go of the pressure.

Deus's wing opens fully, helping him leverage his movement and allowing him to put his whole weight onto his neck. Dannato looks at the golden wing and notices his proximity, but there is one thing in the way, his shoulder. He has one painful choice to make. In a pinch and without consideration for his own suffering, he moves with a nauseating pop and a crack! His shoulder sags backwards at an unnatural angle and with increased mobility. With his limb out of the way and head tucked into a tight choke, he extends his neck and reaches for his target. Deus tightens his grip, noting the newfound slack after the dislocation of his opponent's joint. Dannato's teeth find the outer bone of Deus's wing, close to the connecting tissue on his back.

Opal had never paid attention to Dannato's teeth enough to realize that they had a subtle sharpness to them, so subtle that anyone not paying attention would not notice.

"I bet Era noticed." She thought to herself.

With a roar, the God of Paradise slackens, giving him a brief opening to slither out of the lock. With one limp arm and slightly foggy vision. He mounts Deus, who desperately bucks, trying to get him off his back. With a single working arm, he holds his wing at the soft spot that connects to the angel's back. And with his legs, he tightens his grip with a squeeze of his thighs around Deus's torso.

"Yield!" Dannato yells.

"I will not!" Deus replies.

"I said, Yield!" Dannato pulls at the tissue he holds, making way for the spot his plans to tear.

"I told you, I will not!" Deus bucks harder like a desperate bull trying to dismount its rider.

"You can't say I didn't warn you, big guy." Dannato grips the wing and bears his sharp teeth on the softer connecting tissue connecting the golden wing to his muscular back.

Parity watched from the balcony, a slight green tint flushed her perfectly white skin as she watched the gore play out below.

One bite after another. Through muscle. Through tendons. Through soft tissue. Making art of himself with the blood bath around his lips and dripping down his chin until a sharp wail silences the roaring crowd. Deus falls unconscious. He straddles his bulky figure and spits feathers from his mouth. He stands painted in red and holding one golden wing in his hand, triumphant.

Deus sleeps on the arena floor, and just like the other two Gods, he is now wingless. Dannato steps away and places the severed wing next to the unconscious God. He understands what his wings meant to him and understands the grief he would feel without them. Alas, in battle, everything is allowed, but not everything feels right.

Dannato studies Deus's limp body.

"I'm sorry it had to come to this, again." He says, this time without amusement.

CHAPTER 32

The arena vanished like nothing ever happened. They were all back in the judgment chamber. Neither of the Gods looked tired, dirty, or bloody. There was, however, one slight difference–Deus is missing a very large and significant part of his body, his wing. He sits back in his throne with his arms crossed, avoiding all eye contact with anyone in the room. And, slightly giving his back to the other two Gods. He was throwing an old-fashioned tantrum in good Deus fashion.

Opal noticed his back was not bloody, and the stump was healed. She also noted how the Jury was back in its place, and so is Judas and herself. It was odd, how after so much excitement, they had to return to the serious matters that invoked such excitement.

Parity was now wearing her usual attire again as she spoke without any hints of emotion in that soft voice of hers.

"The judgment of Opal Tempest resumes, and so does the pending decision for a reform." She says. "Dannato, please take the lead." Parity instructs as Deus puffs air from his nose.

"Very well. Let us begin with the reformation of Divine Law and the new Warrior division." Dannato says.

He has his usual spark, although his soft smile disappears whenever he glances over at Deus and his lack of wings. His eyes seem less mischievous with a heavy remorse dulling the red in his irises.

Dannato stands and explains the change that will unravel in the afterlife. His black armor and matching crown adorn him as he speaks. Serenity and confidence exude as he projects to his audience.

"The new Divine Law states as follows: Everyone, regardless of cause of death, is entitled to judgment, including suicide victims and any current Reapers. As we know, Reapers are of utmost importance for the balance of the afterlife, but a new branch was created, and they will be known as Warriors." Dannato snaps his fingers, and an apple appears.

"We have tired of being bystanders, and as the creators of your world, and by proxy humans, we apologize for our oversight. Warriors will act as interventionists in the realm of Medio. They will have the ability to interfere once in a person's lifetime. This will give humans a second chance to reconsider their decision to commit suicide. As this lovely lady has brought to our attention," he gestures towards Opal, "most suicides, with some exceptions such as Henry's, will still come with a sentence. Victims of suicide will be assigned to a branch, either Reaper or Warrior, and serve one-hundred Earth years and then rest in their deserved afterlife, appointed at their judgment."

"Why does suicide require a consequence at all? It's not entirely our fault." Opal objects.

"Great question, dear. We acknowledge that suicide may not be entirely your fault, and with this new system, we will afford humans more autonomy in such decisions. Warriors will inter-vene. And this will have to suffice until we come up with a method to address the Rogues themselves. We still consider human life to be a sacred gift, and Rogues are born from suicides, making suicide victims part of the issue. It's not their fault, or ours, or anyone's, for that matter, but we as Gods think it is fair for them to be selected for service. We thank you and your ways for helping us understand that suicide does not determine a person's overall quality. Suicide victims will have a proper judgment and a choice in service. Now, there is balance." Parity recites.

CHAPTER 33

"**M**iss Opal, in light of recent events, we have weighed your actions, thoughts, soul, and most importantly, your heart." Parity says.

"We have seen who you truly are and what you believe in," Dannato adds.

"And—" an unlikely voice booms from the right.

Deus no longer folds his arms across his chest, and his mouth still pouts. He sits and addresses her fully, a welcomed change in demeanor. He watches her intently and the Reapers in the Jury, and after a deep sigh, he continues.

"You have taught us that all humans are worthy of judgment, and that good and evil come in different shapes and sizes. In order for justice to prevail, we must consider all factors before assigning an afterlife. I will admit you fought valiantly for your beliefs; that was admirable." Deus nods his head, and Opal swore there was a hint of a smile. His pride has finally started to thaw ever so slightly.

The Jury of Reapers that line the sides of the space stand in unison. One by one, they lift the hoods of their cloaks, revealing their faces. Young and old. Women, men, and children. Different shades of skin colors and an array of ethnicities line the seats. The

Gods, the Jury, and the Universe are finally ready to give their final verdict.

Judas watches the scene in awe, but his attention is split between this moment that surely will make history and the waves of Opal's hair and the love that resides in her eyes for others. The warmth of her soul keeps him watching her as she lights the flame of hope in the hearts of others.

"Opal Tempest, you are hereby declared good in nature. We have decided that you deserve the opportunity to earn salvation in my dominion. You will rest in Purgatory after your sentence with the possibility of one day reaching Paradise." The Goddess of Balance speaks.

Her judgment was fair, and she could live her eternity at peace, even in purgatory, knowing that she made a difference. She could keep fighting without remorse, knowing that every soul in the world and in this chamber would have an appropriate judgment. She didn't quite understand how Purgatory worked. She had heard that it was a place of constant tests, but it didn't matter to her. She was happy and at peace.

"Will I continue to be a Reaper?" She asks.

"You have proven to be overqualified for that position, dear. You will be honored as the first official Warrior to serve in the afterlife. You will be allowed and trained to keep interfering now with a guideline of your own, and you will be entrusted to train others just as Judas trained you." Dannato says with a snap of his finger, both an apple and a bushel of grapes appear.

He throws a grape into his mouth and bites his apple at the same time. Surprise shapes his face when he recognizes that apples and grapes complement each other. With that, he snaps his fingers again and materializes a platter from thin air with many shining red apples and, to Opal's surprise, multiple bushels of grapes. He grasps the fruits and starts snacking on them. After the duel and the events after it, something was brewing in his head. He couldn't stop thinking of the contents of the letter Opal had handed to him. He had all the intentions of exploring the endless possibilities that would arise from the deity Era.

Judas hands Opal her scythe. The weight of it is comfortable in her hands. Pearl vibrates with the contact; now they both feel whole again.

"Hey, girly, turns out we'll get to keep kicking ass together." Pearl bends at her base and pats Opal's head with the flat side of her blade.

"Is that supposed to happen?" Deus asks the other two Gods.

"At this point, I don't know." Dannato answers.

Parity announces the case closed, and everyone in the room observes as Opal celebrates. Her laugh lights up the space and infects the Reapers, who cheer along with her.

CHAPTER 34

The following days were full of organized chaos as the new system was put in place. Each Reaper was granted judgment, and some were reassigned as Warriors. All were allowed to interact with each other for the time being, until their sentences resume. A new energy vibrated off of them. Most of them showed their faces and held their chins up. This was refreshing to Opal; she met lots of people who had similar experiences to hers. Some went into long tangents of how their life on Earth was when they were alive, a lot of them were from different time periods than Opal. This made her wonder how many times they tried to make their sentences longer to avoid the boiling cauldrons in the Underworld? Some Reapers went into vivid detail about their experiences with Rogues on Earth and in the afterlife. Her conversations with the group turned into that of a support group, they shared experiences until she saw the one person she was really interested in getting to know walk through the door into the Reaper hall.

The Gods had made a hall for Reapers to sit and wait while their judgments were taken care of. It was similar to Opal's Reaping room, the one where Judas had trained her for the first time. This one had stone walls and even taller ceilings. In the center was an equally towering wooden door, and through it walked a man who once bore an infinite frown, who was now smiling at the girl who waited for him with excitement. Judas finally attended his own judgment. He was the last one to do so. With that, Opal had an avalanche of pressing questions. However, she decides to wait to not overwhelm him. She approached him with the biggest smile she could muster, making her cheeks hurt. She waited for him to start speaking, hoping he would open up without her prodding, but she was wrong. Reapers one by one began opening rifts and saying goodbye, as the time to restart their sentences was approaching. Only until the room was empty and they were the last two did they start talking.

"How did it go?" She asks.

"It was fine, I got pretty much what I thought I would." Judas shrugs.

"Purgatory? Oh my God! Twins!" She bumps his shoulder with her own. "How do you feel?"

"Surprisingly–" he takes a long look at her, "at peace. I think it's fair. It was time someone shook things up around here." He shoves her shoulder, too. "We were so lost in our own suffering that we never bothered to think that something might be wrong." He admires how her little eyes light up when he speaks. His hands feel somewhat empty without hers in them.

"One hundred cows! I would give her father an infinite amount of cows and lumber. Anything he'd want, I would give." He thought.

"It took a small–" Judas grabs her hand and pulls her into him, "and sassy girl to kick some sense into us." His smile beams, and she relishes the sight of it. He holds her with his hands on her waist, and her chin tilted up towards him.

The Gods had stated that once everyone was judged, Earth's timeline would restart where it left off. Without Reapers in operation, it was only wise for the Gods to pause time altogether. When time resumes, Reapers and Warriors will complete their sentences in solitude; that part did not change. Except for Opal, who has a certain friend who is good at stirring up trouble.

"So how old are you?" She asks quickly and wraps her arms around his neck before she loses the nerve to do so. He's quite tall, and Opal stretches a bit so that she is able to clasp her hands together behind his neck. He notices and opts to carry her off the floor.

"I was twenty-nine when I died. Is that too old for you?" He asks while their faces are dangerously close.

"I'm assuming you were alive a very long time before I was, but I think we might get to discuss the details of that later. But, no, you aren't too old for me." She sighs at the sight of the red clock inching towards the start of time. "Well, time starts soon. Any last words?" Her feet still hover off the ground, she levitates a bit to help off load her self until she sees his frown after noticing the change in weight. They still gaze into each other. They both have so many feelings and questions, but not enough time, at least not right now.

"Thank you." He bows his head forward so that their foreheads touch.

The red clock is a few seconds from hitting time.

"There is the possibility that we might get to see each other again, possibly in Paradise." She allows him to rest his forehead on hers, and she closes her eyes, enjoying the interaction. "I wouldn't hate the idea of spending eternity getting to know you." She smirks.

"I wouldn't hate that either." He winks at her and finally slowly lowers her back to the floor.

Together, they swing their scythes and open two separate rifts. Their faces are illuminated with hues of pinks and purples as their gazes brand their souls with longing for the time they might get to see each other again. The red clock hits time. Panic rises in Judas, and without thinking, just as he reached for her door on their first training day, he reached for her arm. With force and yet a gentle tug, he pulls her back into him and dips his face into hers.

"Opal—may I?" He asks permission.

"You may." She says.

He fully leans in. Their lips collide in a tender embrace. Like the sun kissing the ocean during a sunset: brief, beautiful, and bound to happen again.

Opal lets go of the embrace, her face threatening to crumble, and jumps straight through her rift without looking back, afraid that she'll never leave him behind if she were to do so. She faces her sentence with her heart in her hand and her friend on her back.

"I forgive *me*."

Echoes after every step of every day, leading her closer and closer to that sunset she longs for once again.

CHAPTER 35

Epilogue

A large, perfect circle opens, connecting the beautiful, eternal sunset of Era's home with the eternal darkness of Dannato's domain. The swirls at the edges of this rift have an array of multiple colors dancing: pinks, purples, blues, and black. She walks through wearing a silky black dress, the fabric perfectly clinging to her curves. She wore her long white hair down, which swayed with every step she took towards the depths of the Underworld.

The Underworld is cold compared to her home. She knew there were levels to it. In this particular one, mountains of black and grey rock create a labyrinth towards an extremely gothic castle at the top of the tallest mountain. There was red lighting striking around, but no rain. The smell of sulfur and sour apples filled her nose. This place was quiet, and when she listened closely, she could hear the faraway sounds of yelling—the sound of human agony. A small shiver works its way up her back, but the pep in her step brightens at the sight of a tall, dark-haired man.

"Dannato." She curtsies.

"Era." He takes her hand and plants a kiss on the back of it.

"Allow me the pleasure to give you a tour of my home."

"Already? You do know this is only our first date." She winks at him.

"I'm aware, but your letter has intrigued me in unholy ways." He gently leads her hand to the bend of his elbow. His ruby red eyes sparkle in bright contrast with all the black surrounding his domain. He roams the angles of her face and the shade of grey of her skin, until he is distracted by the bright red on her lips. He leads her towards his home.

"I assume we'll have dinner first, before we speak about business matters, correct?" She snaps her fingers, and instantly, a glass of red wine appears in her hand.

Era was not aware that her powers still worked outside her realm; this was a welcome realization.

"Of course, madam. After all, I am a gentleman." He snaps his fingers and makes Era's glass disappear from her hand and reappear in his. He inspects the liquid and takes a sip. "What do you think about playing a part in the human afterlife?" He asks as he returns the glass to her hand and steadily strides towards his castle.

"How exactly?" She sips the crimson in her crystal glass and notices that her wine tastes slightly sweeter than before.

"You did such a great job with Opal, I thought you might be interested in participating with the new division of Warriors and possibly Rogues," Dannato says. He levels his eyes with hers, gauging her playful reaction.

"I don't work for free, no matter how handsome you are." She flips her hair, pointing her chin away from him.

Their steps come to a halt. With delicate fingers, he grasps her chin and leads her face towards him.

"Now, now. Who said it would be for free?" He lets go of her chin and resumes their stroll, leading her towards her new home.

ABOUT THE AUTHOR

Hello, P.R. Miguel here. I am excited to introduce myself as a new author with my debut book titled Rogue Reaper. Through storytelling and imagination, I strive to discuss multiple concepts and difficult themes that I value tremendously. I hope that these narratives can spark healthy conversations about sensitive subjects. Being an avid reader for most of my life and having a vivid imagination prompted me to write my own book. Becoming an author has always been an aspiration of mine, and it never crossed my mind that one day I would actually achieve this until writing for fun turned into something I thought was worth sharing.

I am beyond excited to share the daunting and challenging journey of publishing with you. As a new author, I do not have access due to personal challenges to traditional or professional editing; that being said, I poured my heart into this book and ensured multiple rounds of editing, beta-reader feedback, and lots of proofreading were completed. Although it may not be perfect, I tried my very best to put out my best work for your enjoyment. I have multiple projects at works, and I can't wait until my audience reads it all. Thank you for taking the time to get to know me.